born too

short

The Confessions of an Eighth-Grade Basket Case

BY DAN ELISH

Simon Pulse
New York   London   Toronto   Sydney   Singapore

First Simon Pulse edition September 2003

Copyright © 2002 by Dan Elish

SIMON PULSE
An imprint of Simon & Schuster
Children's Publishing Division
1230 Avenue of the Americas
New York, NY 10020

Also available in an Atheneum Books for Young Readers hardcover edition.
Designed by Abelardo Martínez
The text of this book was set in New Century Schoolbook.

Printed in the United States of America
10 9 8 7 6 5 4 3 2

The Library of Congress has cataloged the hardcover edition as follows:
Elish, Dan.
Born too short: the confessions of an eighth-grade basket case / by Dan Elish.
p. cm.
"A Richard Jackson book."
Summary: Thirteen-year-old Matt is so envious of his best friend Keith that he wishes things would go badly for him, and when Keith's fortune changes while at the same time Matt finds his first true girlfriend, Matt is overcome with guilt.
ISBN 0-689-84386-0 (hc.)
[1. Best friends—Fiction. 2. Friendship—Fiction. 3. Jealousy—Fiction. 4. Interpersonal relations—Fiction.] I. Title
PZ7.E4257 Me 2002
[Fic]—dc21   2001022987
ISBN 0-689-86213-X (Simon Pulse pbk.)

For Andrea

One

Ever see a picture of your best friend's teeth on the side of a bus?

I have. It was the first day of eighth grade, a breezy September afternoon. One of those days when the New York City air actually smelled fresh. Keith and I were on the corner of 79th and Madison on the way home from school.

"Hey, dude!" he said.

"Hey, what?" I looked up (*up* because I'm a good five inches shorter than he is. But more on that later).

"See!" Keith went on.

He jabbed a thumb at the 79th Street crosstown.

"Check me out!"

Keith is so studly they used his smile in a toothpaste ad. A pretty impressive sight. I mean, his teeth are pathologically straight. And his gums are pink like the center of a medium steak. I could see why he landed the job—a dentist would crawl on his stomach across a bed of staples to get a peek inside a mouth like that.

"Not bad," I said. "You've got movie-star gums."

Keith brushed a hand through his hair— he likes to do that because it's long and blond and makes him look sort of like a British rock star. You might say that Keith is a little bit conceited. But he has the goods to back it up. At the time, he had already made out with more girls than I have toes.

"Hmmm," he said, and scratched his chin. "And when I'm in the movies, Matt, you'll be a famous musician. Selling out Madison Square Garden."

It was a nice thing to say, I have to admit it. But Keith is like that—for every compliment he gives himself he throws in another for me. Sort of a buy-one, get-one-free kind of deal. Anyway, I was trying not to blush. The one thing I'm really good at is guitar. Classical. Not that I'm terrible at everything else. With the exception of French, I get decent grades—B's, mostly. I played third base in Little League. Hit .287 (plus I walked a lot on account of my height). I guess you could say that I wasn't a loser. I just didn't feel like a certifiable winner, either.

"The Garden?" I said. "Classical guitarists don't play there."

"Hey, you never know," Keith said. "I guess we've got to ace eighth grade before we conquer the world, right?"

"Right!"

"You know what? I have a strong feeling that this year is gonna be the coolest!"

"Damn straight." Hey, who was I to say this year wouldn't be the coolest?

That's when Keith started this sort of good-bye ritual we had.

"You rule," he said.

"No, you rule," I replied.

"No, *you!*"

"No, *you!*"

"You!"

"You!"

You get the idea. It went on like that for a while. Then we traded some high fives and I took a step down 79th Street.

Looking back, I think that if I had only walked a little faster and been out of earshot before Keith called to me, I would've made it home with no notable rise in my Jealousy Quotient. As it was, I heard every last word.

"Hey," he said. "Who do you think I should call for this weekend? Jane or Allison?"

I thought it over. Jane is an out-and-out babe. Allison, too. But then I remembered Allison's snot-nosed, I'm-better-than-everybody attitude.

"Jane," I said.

"You think?" Keith asked.

"Definitely."

"Cool, dude. Thanks."

And with that my buddy took off, leaving me standing alone on the corner—standing alone eating a walloping portion of his I'm-already-dating-and-you-aren't dust. Well, okay—I had dated a little. That summer at camp I even had my first kiss. But given that the kisser was a buck-toothed girl with chapped lips named Hannah Shaddock and the kiss itself clocked in at under three seconds . . . well, it didn't exactly count for much. The point was this: What was a guy to do when his best friend was Keith Livingston, a stud/athlete/Adonis who went through girls faster than most guys riffle through their top drawer for a clean pair of socks?

Sure, I'm good at music. I have what my mom calls "a sensitive side." But what did that get me when my voice was cracking and I had been stalled at five one and a half for a year?

I mean, how could I wow girls with my mind-blowing classical guitar technique with Keith Livingston in the room flashing dimples as deep as the potholes in the West Side Highway?

I talked to my dad about it. He's a shrink, so he can be a pretty good listener. He told me that growing up is hard and that my day in the sun would come. He said that life is funny—that things you want often come when you aren't thinking about them. Well, that seemed confusing. If the only way to get something you want is to *not* think about it, how is it possible to *not think* about that thing you want? Don't ask me. All I knew was that the situation sucked. Keith had been my best friend since first grade. I mean, we were six when we met. Six! We had sleepovers, play dates, park dates—you name it. We dropped water balloons off my apartment terrace (Sixteen stories!!! Yes!!!). We made crank phone calls. One of our favorites was to get the phone book and call guys with the last name "Chas." "Hi, is this Mr. Chas?" one of us'd say (usually Keith). "Uh, yes . . . ," the guy'd reply sort of cautious. Then we'd shout: "Hi, Chas—how's your ass?" Stupid, yeah—but it made us laugh. There was more to our friendship than playing dumb pranks, though. Keith was like family. The summer between fifth and sixth grade I stayed at his country house in Vermont for a whole month. When his folks went to Europe a year ago he crashed with us for a week. I loved him almost as much as my own parents. More, sometimes.

But as I walked home that day, I knew that, excepting a major growth spurt that would turn me into some sort of eighth-grade Harrison Ford, hanging out with him that year was going to test the limits of my sanity.

Sure, Keith was my best buddy.

But I was beginning to hate him.

Two

As you may have figured, Keith and I are born-and-bred New Yorkers. I live over on the east side and Keith across Central Park on the west. Like many city kids, we go to private school—ours is Hannaford. Not a bad place. It's coed, about sixty kids in a grade. (No dress code, thank God.) Our principal, Ms. Finkle, is always telling us how we're getting one of the best educations in the United States. Sometimes I even believe her.

Can you say, "Homework?" Well, say it a hundred times fast and you'll get some sort of idea about what a Hannaford kid has to do. Papers, reports, tests—the whole nine yards. I mean, some hyper kids started to stress out about college as early as seventh grade. But I know from Emily, my older sister, that most colleges don't look at your grades until high school. So I figured it was at least a year before I had to get nervous.

Hannaford also prides itself on this terrific arts program. We have an orchestra for the fifth and sixth grades. (Ever heard a car alarm at three A.M.? Well, that's what a bunch of eleven-year-olds sound like massacring Mozart. I should know because I played second clarinet for a while in fifth grade until my total lack of ability became so evident that even my mom noticed. Which is when I started to really get into guitar.) Anyway, Hannaford's the place to be if you're a creative type. Students are encouraged to play instruments, write poems, create dance pieces—just about anything as long as it doesn't include sex or drugs.

A couple of weeks into eighth grade Keith got an idea.

"Dude!" he said. We were on the way to science class. "This is what we need to do: start a band."

"A band?" I said.

"Sure!" Keith declared. Aside from being the best-looking guy in the grade and the best athlete, Keith thought he was this superhot musician. All he had mastered in one year of lessons as far as I could tell was how to crank

8

his amp to ten and play loud. But it must've sounded good to him. "I've already got the name: 'The Electric Face.'" He smiled. "Awesome, huh?"

Who was I to say it wasn't awesome?

So The Electric Face was born. With Keith and me manning the guitars, we recruited Bobbie Alina to play the bass and another girl, Gina Parsons, to play drums. For the next month we met every Saturday afternoon in a tiny back room at Keith's place (one of those super-old West Side apartments that actually has a staircase) and pounded out really loud, ultra-raw renditions of the Stones, Springsteen, Nirvana, Madonna—whatever. Keith's folks probably suffered permanent hearing loss, but we had fun.

Too bad we sucked. Before we realized just how bad we really were, we got a gig playing a seventh-and-eighth-grade Halloween dance. Luckily they couldn't round up enough chaperones and it was canceled, saving us from certain public humiliation. The next day we did a favor for the collective eardrums of the universe and The Electric Face disbanded. My teacher, Mr. McMorris, thought I was ruining my classical technique by playing bar chords on steel strings, anyway.

But while I was happy to forget about being a rock star, Keith was just beginning. He spent Thanksgiving vacation writing these loud, generally awful songs. The Electric Face had actually learned one original—by me, if you can believe it—a little punk rock ballad I wrote one night called "He Was Short." The chorus went like this:

He was short but the chicks adored him.
So much that the dudes abhorred him.
Yes, he put the babes on life support.
They loved him because he was short.

Wishful thinking? Maybe. But the song had a good groove. Really, it did. Good or bad, "He Was Short" was Lennon and McCartney compared with the trash Keith was turning out. With titles like "I'm a Thick, Hot Tuna, Mamma" and "She Taught Seventh-Grade English and I Loved Her," let's just say Jon Bon Jovi wasn't sweating bullets. For starters, Keith only knew four chords. *Four*—A, E, D, and B. Second, his rock-star hair didn't help him sing on key. Third, lyrics weren't exactly his strong suit. When I played him the first draft of "He Was Short," he suggested I rhyme the word "creature" with "sheet fur."

Sports? Yes.

Girls? Definitely.

Schoolwork? Not bad, either. (Keith made a solid B+.)

But music? Sorry. My best bud had no talent. As in none. Zero. *Nada.* Zip.

He didn't hear it that way, though. Or if he did, he didn't care. He was determined to be the next big thing. I just didn't know how determined until one day in homeroom the first week of December. I think we were comparing the Knicks to the Nets. I was arguing for the underdog but Keith is a Knicks man. Anyway, we were discussing Jason Kidd's jump shot—at least that's what I *thought* we were discussing—when out of the blue, like he had just thought of it, Keith said, "I'm thinking of writing a musical."

I'd be lying if I said I wasn't surprised.

"A rock musical," he added. "Cool, huh?"

A rock musical? No way could he pull it off.

"What'll your show be about?" I asked Keith.

"Well," he said, warming to the subject, "I figured I'd do something big . . . sort of like *Rent.*" Then he rubbed a hand through his hair and added, "But better."

Ever since his mom had taken us to see

the show at the end of sixth grade, Keith had been a diehard *Rent*aholic. I'm not a big musical fan myself. When I was a kid, my sister played her *Annie* and *The Sound of Music* CDs so often I thought I'd have to be hospitalized for sugar shock. Still, I have to admit that *Rent* has its moments. It's based on the opera *La Bohème* and is about these guys who live in the East Village, do some drugs, and fall in and out of love. At the end of the show, this girl with AIDS miraculously comes back to life and everyone jumps up and sings like they've just hit the jackpot on *Who Wants to Be a Millionaire?* It's a little hard to swallow. But the good outweighs the bad. Anyway, Keith knew the lyrics cold and played all of the songs on guitar. Since most of them called for more than four chords, I don't have to tell you how they sounded. But since I'm a good friend I kept my mouth shut.

"Okay," I said. "What's your story going to be?"

"Well," Keith said. "Figured I'd base it on *Romeo and Juliet.*"

That was logical. We had read the play in English class at the end of seventh grade. But then I thought of something. Thanks to my sister I had picked up a lot of musical theater trivia over the years. My brain was cluttered with raindrops, roses, and the occasional kitten whisker.

"Wait a second," I said. "Isn't *West Side Story* based on *Romeo and Juliet?*"

Keith wrinkled his brow, thinking it over. For a minute I thought the whole thing was going to die right there. But then he flashed that golden grin of his.

"But did *West Side Story* have rock music?"

"No," I had to admit.

Keith smiled big—big enough for the side of a bus.

"Then *no problemo,* dude."

Apparently, Dr. Lester, the junior high theater teacher, had *no problemo,* either. Not only did he give his approval, he agreed to direct and help Keith adapt the script! Assuming Keith could finish it, the whole thing was slated to be performed the first week of April. Sometimes I think that if old Dr. Lester hadn't been so encouraging, none of the crazy stuff ever would have happened. Because, let's face it, it was on opening night of *Star Crossed* that everything went nutso. That's when I made those crazy wishes.

"Hey, Matt," Keith said to me just before Christmas break. "This time next year, I might be on Broadway."

We were back in homeroom. Again, I had

thought that the number one topic of conversation was going to be basketball. But Keith slapped my back to make his point: "Broadway, dude!"

All right, I admit it. My Jealousy Quotient was acting up pretty good—sort of like the creature that explodes out of that guy's stomach in the first *Alien* movie. I mean, I was the one with musical talent! So much talent that Miss Antonucci, our music teacher, had just nominated me for a summer scholarship to the Aspen Music Festival in Colorado. If anyone should be writing a show based on *Romeo and Juliet,* it should've been me. I mean, what about "He Was Short"?

Still, I stayed cool. Instead of telling Keith how I really felt, I sucked it up, flashed a big thumbs-up, and dispensed a congratulatory high five.

"Damn straight!" I said. "Broadway!"

Hey, it was the least I could do.

After all, he was my best friend.

Three

Part of me expected my bud to lose interest in the show and let the whole thing slide. You know, get a song or two into it, then blow it off.

Boy, was I wrong.

Lose interest? *Not!* I mean, you should've seen it. Overnight, my pal became this turbocharged writing machine. Seriously. Over Christmas break he got up every single morning to work.

I mean, *every single day!!!*

Which I admit made me feel a little weird. It was the first time in the history of Keith-Mattitude that we were separated. Not that I didn't have things to keep me busy. I had my own practicing (two hours a day). Some vacation homework too. Still, I missed

Keith. Not to mention that I was majorly curious about what he was writing.

I got a sneak preview at his place a couple of days before Christmas. The minute I made it down the hall, Keith whipped out his guitar and began to sing his opening number.

> *"Romeo! Oh, Romeo!*
> *There's a dance—you gotta go, go, go!*
> *It's a chance you just can't blow, blow, blow!*
> *'Cause Juliet, yes Juliet!*
> *Will be the chick—to get, get, get!*
> *With hair that's so brunette, 'nette, 'nette!"*

Not to be vain or anything, but I saw about a thousand ways to make the song better. And okay, I admit it: Deep down I was sort of hoping that Keith would crawl across the floor, lick my high-tops, and beg me to help. But he already had Mr. Lester's help.

"What do you think?" Keith asked.

I'd known him long enough to know when he was looking for encouragement as opposed to an honest opinion. So I said, "Hey, sounds great!" and left it at that.

Whatever. To tell the truth, last winter I was more caught up with the state of my love life. Forget Romeo and Juliet's. I had hoped to parlay my minor summer success with Hannah Shaddock into eighth-grade pay dirt. By that I mean, have a real, live girlfriend. One I could truly kiss. Make out with, even. Unfortunately, girls were to me like songwriting talent was to Keith.

Can you spell L-O-S-E-R?

In short (no pun intended), I was getting nowhere. Not that I didn't have crushes. I had millions. The trouble was that none of the girls I liked crushed me back. And what made it worse was the progress of my buddy, the blond Don Juan. Keith was switching partners so quickly I practically needed a chart to keep track!

Here's a list (just the first half of eighth grade!!!).

Nancy Williams
Mariana O'Connell
Gina Parsons (our drummer)
Barbara Oakes
Lynn Larsen

Sickening, huh?

Until . . . well, until something weird happened. And by weird, I mean, *weird!!!* See, just when I was thinking that Hannah Shaddock

17

would be the absolute limit of my lifelong sexual experience, lightning struck.

Are you sitting down?

Because for a brief period of time that winter—from January 15th until February 21st, five weeks, two days, to be exact—I actually did have a girlfriend!

Yesss!!!!!!!!

Not that Abigail Warriner and I liked each other much. We got thrown together at one of Peter Brown's spin-the-bottle parties—one of those "who's-left-over-after-the-people-who-really-like-each-other-pair-up" sorts of things. And we were a strange match, mostly because Abigail was about a foot taller than me. She wasn't bad-looking, though. From certain angles she reminded me of Jennifer Aniston. Then again, from other angles she looked like a giraffe. Given our height difference, I had a really good view of her neck. But once we got in a dark closet and kissed, it didn't much matter. I just stood on my tippy toes and let my mouth do the rest. Who cared if she was tall enough to play small forward for most NBA teams?

I had finally made out!!!

Yes!!!!

Too bad our hot romance crashed to a halt over Washington's birthday—the long weekend. I was in my room practicing guitar when my mom knocked on the door.

"Yeah," I called, sort of irritated because I take my practicing pretty seriously. Like I said, two hours a day.

Next thing I knew, Mom stuck in her head with this demented grin on her face—the kind that means she thinks something is extra-specially cute.

"You've got company," she said.

Before I could say a word, in walked Abigail. She was wearing blue jeans and this tight white blouse. She looked nice. Smelled good, too. Sort of like a soap commercial. It crossed my mind that maybe she had bathed just for me. And when she sat down on my bed and began to fidget with my pillow, I got my hopes up even more. See, she seemed sort of nervous, uncomfortable. I had this quick little thought that she was working up the courage to ask me to take off my shirt! Embarrassing, but true. I even envisioned us playing a game of strip Monopoly. (I had heard that college kids do that.) Like, "You landed on St. Charles. That'll be four hundred bucks and your bra." That sort of thing.

Boy, was I wrong. It turned out my grossly underdeveloped chest (no muscle tone, two hairs) was the last thing on Abigail's mind.

After a minute or two of chitchat, she finally got to the point.

"Look, Matt," she said. "I don't think this thing we have is working."

I had so convinced myself that we were about to be naked that I admit I wasn't exactly sure what she was saying.

"This thing?" I said.

"Yeah . . . this relationship."

Silence.

"You know," she said. "*Our* relationship."

Suddenly, my heart was pounding—hard. Somehow I didn't think any shirt-removal requests would be coming down the pike.

"Oh . . . ," I said.

"It's not working," she repeated.

"Not working?" I squeaked, eventually.

At that point, Abigail proceeded to give me a sort of rehearsed speech. I don't claim to remember all of it. Just snippets.

"We're too young to make a serious commitment," she said.

Loose translation: I was too short for her to make a serious commitment with.

"I admire your talent so much, but I need some time to myself," she said.

Loose translation: "I admire your talent, but you're a dwarf."

"I guess I see myself with someone more outdoorsy," she said.

Yeah, like Keith.

As you can guess, not quite strip Monopoly. Anyway, it didn't take long before there wasn't much else to say. That night I nearly cried. I knew I didn't really like her. But it still felt lonely.

Even worse, this was right about the time *Star Crossed* started rehearsals. Suddenly, it seemed like Keith's show was the only thing anyone could talk about. Every time I turned around it was Keith, Keith, KEITH!!! For starters, about half our class was in the thing. I didn't try out. But I painted this backdrop of downtown Verona one Saturday afternoon. I also hung lights. But it was weird. Keith never asked me to help with the music. Or to play in the band. Yeah, he knew that Mr. McMorris had told me not to touch an electric guitar but still . . . my bud could've asked, right? Even worse, he lined up these three tenth graders to play. Which meant that he was suddenly hanging with kids from high school.

ARRRRGGGHHHHHH!!!!!!!

But remember Dad saying: Things you want often come when you aren't thinking about them? Well, pretty soon it was late March, a week before the show. The first signs of spring were in the air and all that. Emily was home from boarding school, and Mom made plans for us to have brunch at my aunt Esther's. Now, these events are not the highlights of my year. You know how it is— you sit at a table listening to grown-ups talk about the decline of modern liberalism or communism in the police department—that sort of thing. But a half hour or so after we arrived, the doorbell rang.

"Oh," Aunt Esther said. "I invited the Robinsons for coffee. I hope that's all right."

Turned out to be better than all right. In stepped this middle-aged couple . . . then a five-year-old boy . . . and then . . .

A vision!

An angel!!

My savior!!!

Katie Robinson!!!!

When I shook her hand I felt this series of little electric shocks run up my arm. I think I got gooseflesh. My knees wobbled. Seriously. Katie's hand was so soft, I could've held it forever.

You know how white the snow is when it first falls on the city streets? Before it gets blackened over by car exhaust? That's how white her skin was. And you know how blue the sky can be on a sunny day when the wind blows the smog out to the ocean? That's how blue her eyes were. Her nose was a little button. Her blond hair was on par with Keith's. But best of all . . .

She was short!!!

Pushing five feet, give or take an inch. My height! Anyway, Katie was a girl I could look in the eye.

Yes!!!!!!!

For a moment I was so nervous, I pretended to be interested in one of my uncle Saul's stories about the garment industry. But Aunt Esther is cool. Pretty soon I felt a tap on my shoulder.

"Matt," she said, "why don't you show Katie to the kitchen? Maybe she'd like some dessert."

I don't have to tell you how fast I got to my feet. I'm not sure what we talked about but it seemed we had everything in common. I mean, *everything*.

"You like the Rolling Stones?" she said. "My God! So do I!"

Like that.

Better still, before we left my aunt took out Uncle Saul's old guitar and called on me to give a little concert. The love gods must've been smiling 'cause I ripped through a piece by Andrés Segovia like my hands were on fire. And I mean on fire!!! Man, I was good! Keith Livingston step aside! Matthew Greene is dazzling the most beautiful girl in town!! When I was through, Katie was grinning like a madwoman. As we got our coats to leave, I had a stroke of absolute, certifiable genius—at least it seemed like it at the time. See, I decided to invite her to Keith's show the following weekend. What could be better than making an entrance in front of my entire grade—no, most of the junior high—with a hot babe as my date?

What better way to get back at Keith for freezing me out?

Yes! Yes!! Yes!!!

Matt Greene—the manly man!

Matt Greene—Babe Master!!

Matt Greene—the studliest of the wudliest!!!

Still, I was nervous. Make that terrified. I mean, I'd never asked a girl out before—not really. Hannah Shaddock and I had met at a camp dance. And Abigail and I had sort of fallen together like we were participants in some twisted scientific experiment set up to research the relationship between giants and midgets. But thank God for Aunt Esther.

"You two seem to be having such fun," she said. "Why don't you exchange numbers?"

I couldn't speak. But Katie came through—big-time. No hesitation. Just this great smile.

"Sure," she said.

I was floored.

Floored!

But that night I worked up the guts and forced myself to the phone. What I said isn't important. But her answer was—a simple, sweet "yes." I hung up and practiced dunks on my Nerf basketball for a full hour.

KATIE ROBINSON SAID YES!!!

Take that, Keith!!!

Say there, fella. . . . Whose chart is filling up now????

Four

Chart? Hah!

Looking back, I guess I was too cocky. A little too eager to show up my best buddy. Fate had sent me my dream date. But Mother Nature was about to completely screw it up.

The scene was this: It was Friday night—or should I say, opening night—and I was standing outside the Hannaford auditorium, dressed in a blue blazer, khaki pants, and loafers. I had used my dad's Speed Stick, rubbed about half a tube of Clearasil on this zit on my forehead, and combed my hair until my arm hurt. (I have this ultra thick hair that tends to sit on my head like a dead bear cub unless I comb it way down.) Anyway, I was duded up, ready for action. Ready to meet my big, hot date.

Right next to me was this bright red poster:

ONE NIGHT ONLY
April 2 at 7:30
THE WORLD PREMIERE PERFORMANCE

KEITH LIVINGSTON'S ROCK OPERA
(based on William Shakespeare's *Romeo and Juliet*)

STAR CROSSED

I have to admit, I thought (make that *hoped*) only a few classmates would show up. But like I said, Keith's show had captured the school's imagination. Hannaford was covered with flyers, and Ms. Finkle had made an announcement in the upper school assembly. Now it seemed like everybody had turned out for the event—students, parents, teachers. I even saw Herman, the custodian, holding hands with Rachel, the nurse. They had made a date of it or something. The lobby was buzzing like a Broadway opening.

You're probably thinking that this obscene turnout sent my J.Q. into warp drive. But the truth was that I was more a weird combination of totally pumped and totally petrified. Don't forget: Katie Robinson was my first real date. That afternoon, Mom had tried to calm my nerves by telling me about the first time she went out with Dad—about how they went to Coney Island and ate hot dogs and rode the Cyclone and held hands on the Boardwalk. About how four months later they were engaged. Straight out of a Woody Allen movie. Well, it turned out that my big night didn't come wrapped in a ribbon with a big Hollywood ending and a cheesy ballad sung by Mariah Carey. Nope, my sound track was straight from *The Blair Witch Project*. From the minute I arrived, let's just say that things didn't go entirely according to plan. . . .

Plant yourself in my shoes, standing in front of the auditorium door, trying to look comfortable in your sport coat and tie when *boom!* who should waddle your way but Miss Antonucci, your music teacher. Now, Miss Antonucci's a great musician—she can play piano, guitar, and about four different wind instruments entirely by ear. But she's what my mom politely calls "eccentric." She wears these long skirts with orange socks and is always smacking her lips which she says helps her mouth keep in shape for the oboe. Like Mom says, eccentric. Also, excitable. At least, she was that night.

"Oh, Matty," she called, hurrying toward me. "I'm so, so sorry. I just heard."

Somehow I had the sinking feeling that this didn't have to do with a sudden citywide shortage of orange socks.

"Heard what?" I said.

"You know," she said. "The *news*."

For a second, I thought it had to do with Katie—like she had gotten sick or maybe had had a run-in with a steamroller.

"Aspen," Miss Antonucci continued. She wrinkled her brow. "Didn't anyone tell you?"

"No," I said. Then I gulped. Pretty hard, too. "Didn't I get in?"

The answer was written all over her face. I hadn't. No Aspen Music Festival come summer. I was a guitar whiz, all right—but apparently not quite whizzy enough.

"Oh, Matty!" Miss Antonucci cried, grabbing my lapels. "I'm such a fool. I thought you knew!"

Don't get me wrong—I was upset. But she was so flipped that it seemed like I spent the next five minutes consoling her! I knew Aspen was competitive, but Miss A. had said I'd be a shoo-in. A lock. What would I do over the summer now? Hang by my hands from the shower bar and hope to grow six inches?

"I'm going to write the Aspen committee a letter of protest," Miss Antonucci said.

It was sweet, I guess. But I couldn't see

what good it would really do. I mean, they had already made their decision, right? And then Miss Antonucci reminded me that she had nominated me for some elite summer program in France. To be honest, I was too depressed to listen. Thank God she finally had to go check on the stage mikes for the show. But just before she took off she rubbed her palm through my hair (which had gotten even BIGGER, if you can believe it!!!), leaving me: a) turning about ten shades of purple; and b) with hair like a Dr. Seuss character. Then, just as I was heading for the locker room . . .

Turned out a giant giraffe was on the move! It's true. I was being charged by a wild animal. Looking back, I should've run home right then. Or hidden in the custodian's closet and spent the night inhaling bathroom cleanser. Anything.

What made it worse was that Abigail looked pretty darned good for a giraffe. She had on this tight leather skirt that hugged her hips and showed off her legs. And those legs were long and lean. But Abigail wasn't marching my way to be friendly. Far from it. No, she was coming to show off her date, this ninth grader—a big jock type named Phil or Fred, I forget which. Talk about depressing. Hey, this was the girl who had dumped me, after all. The one who had told me she needed to be *free*. Now I knew what that meant: free to date older, studlier guys. Sure, I didn't really like Abigail. But that sick glow of triumph pasted all over her face filled me with a strong desire to go home, crawl under my bed, and slowly decompose. The last thing I wanted to do was talk to her.

That's because I had this little problem I may have mentioned. With my voice.

It cracked.

Often.

And always at the worst times. I knew, of course, that this was something all boys have to go through. That it's part of the trading-in process from your kid voice to your grown-up one. Still—here I go again—I sure didn't hear Keith's voice cracking like a harpooned seal every time he opened his mouth. Keith's transition into his adult body was probably the smoothest in the history of Western civilization. It's like he went into a phone booth one day after school and emerged five minutes later a full-fledged adult with the low voice and body hair to go with it. He wasn't shaving yet, but he was close.

Abigail and Phil/Fred drew to my side.

"Hi," she said.

"Hi there," I replied.

The "hi" was okay. But the "there"? Put it

this way: Ever been to the Metropolitan Opera? You know, when the soprano hits the high C? Well, that's how it sounded. Except that I'm a guy. As I logged in an eleventh shade of purple, Phil/Fred and Abigail started to grin like a couple of rabid dogs. I would have preferred that they'd caught me whacking off in the lunchroom. Well, *almost*.

"This is Phil/Fred," Abigail said finally.

He shook my hand. "Nice to meet you, Matt."

"Hiya," I said.

That time my voice behaved, thank God.

"Hey, I hear this show is supposed to be great," Abigail went on. She turned to Phil/Fred. "Keith is so talented." Then to me. "Isn't he talented, Matt?"

I clenched my teeth.

"Yeah. He sure is."

Abigail must have known what she was doing. Rubbing it in. That's how girls can be sometimes. Plain nasty. Anyway, I realized in a big, fat hurry that the only way out was to hightail it to the locker room ASAP, recomb my hair, and regroup. But before I could, I happened to glance across the crowded lobby toward the main entrance to the school.

And there she was!

Katie!

And even more beautiful than I'd remembered! So beautiful, I did a double take. She had on a tight black skirt and this slightly low-cut white blouse that pronounced her curves in all the right places. At Aunt Esther's she was a cute girl. Now she looked more like a young woman. Sexy, you know? Maybe on account of the red lipstick and eyeliner.

And just like that, I saw a way to regain a little self-respect. Maybe my hair was messed up. Maybe Aspen had rejected me. Maybe my voice had just cracked. But together, Katie and I would show Mr. Ninth Grade and the hideous giraffe what true love could be. We'd teach them about romance, beauty, and kindness—all that sort of stuff. They'd see that I was a stud to be reckoned with.

I called across the room.

"Katie!"

She looked up but didn't see me. So I waved.

"Katie! Over here!"

Wouldn't you know it? This time she turned and looked in the other direction! Since everyone and their mother had turned out for the show, the lobby was too crowded. She could hear me but couldn't tell where the sound was coming from.

So I tried again . . .

"Katttiiieeeee!"

Crack City—and I'm not talking drugs.

Yep, the soprano was back for an encore. And *boom!*—it seemed like everyone in the lobby stopped talking. Boy, was I embarrassed. Ten more shades of purple. I started sweating like a crazy person. My mouth went dry. I couldn't speak (which under the circumstances may have been the best thing). And Abigail and Phil/Fred? They didn't even try to be civil. No, they grinned like they just won Olympic gold.

"What was that, Matt?" Abigail asked.

See what I mean? Plain nasty.

"Shut up, vile bitch!"

Okay, that's what I *wanted* to say. I think what I really said was more along the lines of . . . well, nothing. I was too busy working on purple shade twenty-two to concentrate on forming words. But in a weird way, my complete and totally humiliated silence worked to my benefit. Since I didn't speak, my voice couldn't crack. And once Abigail and Phil/Fred realized the entertainment was over, they giggled themselves dry and left. Not a second too soon, either. Just as the lobby was beginning to regain its preshow buzz, Katie appeared at my side.

"Hey, there," she said.

"Uh, hi," I stammered.

Miracle! My voice stayed on pitch.

"You look nice," she went on.

I tried to register her words over the sound of my thumping heart. Had she said that I . . . *look nice?*

Apparently, she had. And apparently she was waiting for me to reply.

"You, too," I said, finally.

And Katie smiled. Which gave me the strength to continue.

"Thanks for coming."

"Sure," she said. "I've been looking forward to it."

To tell the truth, I had half expected her to run screaming for the exit after hearing me yodel across the lobby. But it finally dawned on me: If Katie had heard my soprano solo (which, let's face it, she had—I mean, I bet the elevator man at the Empire State Building had heard it and thought someone had jumped), she didn't seem to care!

It's going to be all right, I told myself. It's going to be all right!

What's sad is that I actually believed it— believed that the evening would be a rollicking success, that Katie and I would pick up where we had left off at Aunt Esther's. I could see it all. Afterward, I'd whisk her off to the school courtyard. There I would take her in my arms and kiss her tenderly on the lips. "I love you," she would say. "And I you," I'd reply. And later on? Strip Monopoly.

"Should we go in?" she asked.

"Sure," I said.

And in we went.

Five

If someone asked you to pick the happiest fifteen seconds of your life, would you be able to?

I would. Easy.

I'd pick the fifteen seconds it took Katie and me to walk from the Hannaford School lobby into the auditorium. I know that may sound weird but when you stop to think about it, it makes perfect sense. Because that's when something truly incredible happened. And I mean *incredible!*

Just as we turned toward the double doors, Katie Robinson took my hand!

I repeat: KATIE ROBINSON TOOK MY HAND!

And we didn't just hold hands, palm to palm. We clasped fingers. Did that feel good, having her soft palm next to mine. Like a . . . well, there's really no way to describe it. You've just got to find a girl (or guy) and do it. Then you'll know. But I'll say this: It was even better than my first kiss. (Then again, my first bloody nose was practically better than my first kiss, given that the kisser was Hannah Shaddock.) But that's not the point. What's important is that on that one night, Katie's hand felt so exciting! The reason is I liked her so much.

I read somewhere once that happiness can be fleeting. Or maybe Dad told me. Whatever. The point is that the very instant I set foot inside the auditorium itself—like I said, about fifteen seconds later—my happiness fleeted. Straight out the window. That's because Katie lost interest in me. And you don't have to be a shrink to figure out why. See, standing just a few feet away from us was Mr. Golden Boy himself—Keith "that's my face on a bus" Livingston.

And you've never seen anything like it. He must have stepped into a time machine and turned the knob to 1967. He was wearing these purple bell-bottom blue jeans, black boots, and a blue-and-orange tie-dyed T-shirt. His hair looked like it had been combed by those guys who had made the Scarecrow, Tinman, and

Lion look so sharp in the land of Oz. Talk about locks. He looked like a surfer. Only a surfer with an I.Q. high enough to never actually surf. Anyone else in our grade would've looked like a first-class fool. But Keith had the style and confidence to pull it off.

Still, I have to admit something. At first I didn't give Keith more than a passing glance. See, he was holding hands with a girl. . . . Not that this was so special. I had seen Keith hold hands before. It was the girl in particular who blew me away. 'Cause that girl (are you ready?) was none other than *Wendie Culhane!* Phil/Fred may have been a certified ninth grader. But Wendie Culhane *was in tenth!* Which made me wonder what was going on. I mean, was it "date an eighth grader" night at the high school or something? Anyway, Wendie is one of those all-American types. Long blond hair, blue eyes, long legs. A real girl next door. But a sexy girl next door, if you know what I mean.

Whatever. The next thing I knew Keith was at our side.

"Hi," he said. "You must be Katie."

Keith's general appearance sure wasn't lost on her. Not for a second. For starters, she dropped my hand. I don't think she did it on purpose or anything. She probably didn't even notice I was still in the room. 'Cause the next thing that happened was something I've only heard described in books. Katie's jaw dropped. Really. Like a bag of cement into the East River. Like the *Titanic* taking that final whoosh into the Atlantic. And those cute blue eyes went so wide I thought they were going to slide up and off her forehead. No doubt about it—she had come to the mountaintop and seen Beauty and Truth.

"Hi," she said.

Stammered would be more accurate.

Make that drooled.

"I'm Keith," my buddy said.

At that point, Katie seemed to lose all ability to form complete sentences.

"Gee," she said. "Congratulations . . . I mean, like . . . a whole rock opera! Wow!"

"Oh, it's no big deal," Keith said. "Matt's the real musician. I suppose you've heard him play guitar?"

It was *so* Keith.

"Oh, yeah," Katie said. "I did. But to write a musical—that's really amazing."

Keith waved his hand.

"Like I said, no biggie."

If the conversation had ended there it might have been halfway bearable. The problem was, it didn't. See, it was at just that moment that Keith's folks and four-year-old sister moseyed by, gave him a quick thumbs-up, then moved down the aisle to their seats.

What's so important about that?

Mr. Livingston is a pretty well-known novelist. His best-selling book, *The Unrequited,* is six hundred pages. I haven't read it but my mom told me it's about a veteran of the Korean War who moves to Paris and makes a bundle, then finds religion and gives his money to a blind monk. Great read, huh? My dad told me it began with a two-page sentence. Two pages! That's longer than my English paper on *Of Mice and Men.* Anyway, a few years back Mr. Livingston started to clean up by writing screenplays. And then he hit it big. I mean, BIG! He got Sandra Millicent, the hottest star in Hollywood, to star in his movie, *The Asparagus Itch,* which Keith told me was a political thriller even though it sounded like a movie about a farmer with lice. Filming was scheduled for the summer. And wouldn't you know it? As soon as his dad was out of earshot, Keith started to tell us how he was getting to meet Sandra Millicent in person! He might even have lunch with her in her trailer, he said. Regular soul mates. I don't have to tell you how Katie lapped that up. She lit up like a stoned firefly.

"Sandra Millicent?" she cried. "Ooohhhh! I love her! Can you get me her autograph?"

"I'll see what I can do," said Keith.

Good thing Wendie was there. You could tell she wasn't into sharing Keith with any starry-eyed kid.

"Come on, Keith," she said finally. "Shouldn't you be starting soon?"

Keith glanced at the clock. It was five to eight.

"Oh, yeah," he said. "Good point." Then to us, "Will I see you two at the cast party?"

It was going to be at the Livingstons'.

"Oh, sure!" Katie said.

"We'll be there," I said. "Good luck with the show."

"Yeah, yeah," he said. Then he sort of laughed. "I'm gonna need it."

Even though my J.Q. was percolating I said what a good friend says:

"No way. You're going to do great."

"Sure you are," Katie said.

"No sweat," I said.

Keith smiled and glanced toward the stage where the *Star Crossed* band was tuning up. They looked pretty young for tenth graders—even though one of them had this stringy mustache.

"Well, now or never," he said. "Nice meeting you, Katie. Later, Matt."

"Yeah, later," I said.

He went off with Wendie at his heels. And Katie made no bones about watching him work the crowd, shaking hands like a presidential hopeful all the way down front to the stage. Suddenly, classical guitar—all those hours and hours (and hours!) of practice—seemed like an incredible waste of time. About as sexy as knitting. Or teaching badminton at a girls camp. And my date seemed to agree. On the way to our seats she was jabbering faster than one of those guys who announce horse races. And all about you-know-who. I mean, she didn't even *try* to be subtle.

"I'm so excited to be here!" she said. "A rock opera—based on Shakespeare. And Keith is so cool, isn't he?"

"Oh, yeah," I sputtered. "Very cool."

As we found our seats, I still had some hope that Katie and I could regain the old magic we'd felt at Aunt Esther's. It almost worked, too. Turned out that we had both read *Of Mice and Men* for English class. I managed to get her into a pretty good conversation about George and Lenny. But just as I was about to make a point about John Steinbeck's contribution to American literature (I really was—no fooling), the lights started to dim. And when I looked front and saw Keith strapping on his guitar, I felt jealous as hell. Which is when this twisted thought crossed my mind. I suddenly realized that I had a major ball in my court. And that was this: *Katie was about to actually watch the show!*

I know it sounds simple—even stupid. But here was my logic: After Katie saw how bad *Star Crossed* was, she'd appreciate just how talented *I* was.

Then I'd get her back!

I don't like to admit this. But soon enough, the lights dimmed all the way. It was pitch black. And as the band played the opening chord, I smiled in the darkness. I just couldn't help it.

Come on, I thought as the curtain parted on scene one. Let this show really suck.

Six

I'm not saying that Keith's show was *good*. Because it wasn't. On the other hand . . . well, I've got to be honest: It didn't stink, either. Not the way I assumed it would. He had cut that lousy opening number ("Brunette, 'nette, 'nette") and now, despite the occasional bad line, the lyrics were actually pretty clever. And even though the music was totally basic (I mean, it's hard to do much with four chords), the band sounded tight, and the show as a whole gelled. The sets looked good and the cast was pumped. The audience applauded hard after each song. And at the end, they gave it a standing O. Of course, that could've been because Keith was only in eighth grade and people wanted to be supportive. But hey, a standing O is a standing O where I come from.

And Katie?

"I'm blown away," she gushed at intermission. "This thing is brilliant!"

Then at the final curtain: "Incredible!" she cried. "OhmiGod! OhmiGod!! OH-MI-GAWD!!"

It may surprise you that by that time I sort of agreed with her. *Star Crossed* was no *Rent*. But that didn't mean it wasn't impressive in its own way. In fact, I rose to my feet with the rest of the crowd, proud to be Keith's best friend. Proud of him for pulling the whole thing off. Backstage, I complimented him bigtime. I really did.

But at the cast party it was a different story. See, within a couple of minutes of arriving, my J.Q. came out of hibernation—and I mean like a grizzly who's woken up hungry and in a really, really lousy mood.

It's almost too depressing to tell you how Katie behaved. Oh, sure—she pretended to talk to me now and then. Her parents raised her that well, I suppose. But every time we got going on a conversation, her eyes'd dart this way and that, keeping track of the man of the hour's every move. And when Keith actually passed our way, Katie acted like one of those idiots who camp out before the Academy Awards for a week so they can get a close-up view of a movie star. What made it worse was the fact that my best bud was acting like he'd just picked up his own personal Oscar. Drove me nuts. I mean, I loved the guy but sometimes he just didn't know when to shut up. Was Katie annoyed? No way. Girls love guys who can talk. I might as well have been a sack of fresh manure for all the attention she was paying me.

"You see," Keith told her and a group of other girls a half an hour or so into the party, "I wanted to redefine the rock musical a little bit. You know, to pick up where *Rent* left off."

A guy who could barely play four chords? Picking up where *Rent* left off? *Please.*

"I bet there are Broadway producers who'd be extremely interested," he went on.

"Go for it," Katie said. "Since *Cats* closed, there just aren't any more good shows."

No doubt about it—my friend was riding the ego express, leaning heavy on the throttle. He was bugging me so much, I had to hit the bathroom—not even to pee but to slap some water on my face and get away from it all. Then wouldn't you know it? When I came back to the party, there was Keith—slow dancing with Wendie! And smack in the middle of the living room! But before I could get *too* worked up about it—hey, at least it wasn't Katie—the night took this weird turn. See, there's this guy in our class named Derrick O'Connell. He wasn't a buddy then—more of a "sometimes" friend. Since Keith and I were so tight, I figured I didn't really need anybody else. And to tell the truth, I figured Derrick was a bit too weird to get close to. He's seriously into *Star Trek* and has these red dreadlocks. Word had it that he'd turned his folks' front hall closet into his bedroom. Anyway, the second I returned from the bathroom, Derrick appeared at my side and, just like that, handed me something cold.

"Heya, Matt," he said. "Try this."

I'll cut to the chase. The "this" turned out to be a beer.

"Where'd you get it?"

Derrick glanced over his shoulder. "Abigail's date sneaked in a couple of six packs."

"Oh," I said. "You mean Phil?"

"I thought it was Fred," Derrick said.

I shrugged. I never could get that guy's name straight. Anyway, I had more important things to think about than some jock ninth grader. See, a while ago I'd promised Mom and Dad that I wouldn't take a drink until I was sixteen. But holding that can made me suddenly feel . . . well, grown up—like I was in some sort of commercial. Yeah, I had promised

I'd wait. But given what was happening that evening, it suddenly seemed like the perfect time to start. Who knew? Maybe Katie would find it cool? So I flipped open the top and smelled it.

"You're supposed to drink it," Derrick told me.

"Yeah, I know," I said.

Still, I was sort of nervous. I'm not the sort of kid who disobeys his folks. But they weren't in the room, right? And what was one sip going to do, anyway? Turn me into some sort of alcohol-obsessed delinquent? So before I could change my mind, I brought the can to my lips and went for it.

"Well?" Derrick asked.

The truth? Tasted sort of like lighter fluid. Not that I've drunk a lot of lighter fluid but you get the idea. It was bad. Of course, I didn't tell Derrick that.

"Great," I choked.

"Go ahead and finish it then," Derrick said. "Chug it down."

You're probably thinking I said "no way" and swore off alcohol for the rest of my life. But with a classmate, even a "sometimes" friend, standing there watching, a guy can feel the pressure. Besides, Katie and a girl she knew from Sunday school were standing about ten feet away giggling over something—probably me, for all I knew. I was willing to try anything to get her attention.

So I waited until she happened to look my way (took about a minute!), then did what Derrick told me to do—chugged it down. With each gulp I suppose I got used to the taste a bit more because by the time I got to the bottom of the can it didn't taste like lighter fluid anymore, but cold and refreshing. Derrick seemed to approve.

"Way to go!" he said.

I felt dizzy—but strangely happy. My first brew-doggie! That's a rite of passage, right? Not bad! I shot Katie a glance. Unfortunately, my wild drinking spree hadn't had the intended effect. Instead of crawling across the carpet to worship at my newly cool feet, her eyes were focused on the living room where Keith and Wendie were still slow dancing. But before I could get too bummed out about it something totally unexpected happened. And I mean *unexpected*.

"Hey," Derrick said.

"What?"

Derrick looked both ways to make sure no one was listening.

"Josie Hyde," he said.

"Josie Hyde?" I said.

...he feelings of a girl you're
..., I was so determined to fol-
... land of the lips that I forgot
... For starters, she held me at
...ke I had just gotten back from
...uous stall shoveling or some-
..., her body was about as limber as
... department store mannequin.
...Not! I mean, she was giving me
...othing! And when she looked at
...ought she was going to cry with
... had been smart I would've accepted
...ke a man, gotten the dance over with,
...e home. Like I said, *if* I had been smart.
... that point I was determined to make
...evening turn out the way I wanted if it
... the last thing I did on the planet. *The last*
...ng. So I tried to warm her up with a little
...itchat.

"It's good to be with you tonight," I said.

"Uh, yeah," Katie said. "You, too. Thanks for the show."

Yeah, I know. She was too polite to say anything different. But deep down I knew I was in trouble. In so much trouble that I sort of blocked out reality and went into a little fantasy. 'Cause let's face it, fantasy can be a lot more fun sometimes.

I imagined that Katie liked me—and I

"You heard me."

With that, he nodded across the room. Josie was this girl in the other eighth-grade homeroom who had transferred to Hannaford that year from L.A. She has this long brown hair and a sort of big but regal-looking nose. During the World Series she wore a Dodgers cap every day—backward—even though the Dodgers weren't even in it. Definitely a cool thing. She's pretty in a tomboyish sort of a way. Not to mention on the short side.

"What about her?"

"She thinks you're cute."

I blinked. Then sneaked another peak at Josie. She was chatting with Sheila DeCappio, this slightly punked-out girl with a blond streak in her hair. We had written a report together in fourth grade about exotic African mammals.

"Cool it," Derrick said. "Try not to be so obvious."

"How do you know?"

"Easy. She told me."

"Liar. Why'd she tell you?"

"We're friends."

"You're fooling."

"Nope."

"Seriously?"

"Seriously."

I couldn't help myself and glanced again. I noticed her big brown eyes and long lashes. Also, a slight cleft in her chin. Sure, she was pretty flat-chested but I didn't care about that. Lots of girls were still flat.

The problem was that I still had this burning crush on Katie—a girl who obviously couldn't care less if I crawled down a manhole and spent the rest of my life covered in sewage. But here's the weird part: As much as I wanted to give up on her, I simply couldn't. After all, hadn't Katie and I hit it off at Aunt Esther's? Hadn't she said she'd see the show with me? Then held my hand on that short walk into the auditorium!? She had to like me, right? So what was the problem?

Keith, that's what!

If I could get her far away from him, I might stand a chance! At least that's how I figured it. But how could I do that? Yeah, there was an empty room or two upstairs that I knew about. But what were the odds that Katie would go into one of them with me alone? Zero. Still, just as I was mulling it all over, something even weirder happened. Keith was slow dancing with Wendie Culhane, right? Well, suddenly they were making out! Which wouldn't have been so strange except that it

was so, I d[...]
ents we[...]

[...]
too. W[...]
send me[...]
so maybe[...]
Maybe I was[...]
At the time it s[...]

Before I coul[...]
for Derrick's beer.

"Gimme that," I sa[...]

"What for?"

"Gimme it!"

I took a long gulp.

"What's up?" Derrick aske[...]

"I'm gonna ask Katie to slow[...]

Derrick seemed impressed.

"Feeling a good vibe, huh?"

"Damn straight," I lied. "Watch me.[...]

Pretty macho, huh? Before I could ch[...] my mind, I marched to Katie's side and ask[...] She didn't look too thrilled. In fact, she sort o[...] frowned and glanced over her shoulder toward the door. But I guess her good breeding kicked in 'cause she finally shrugged and let me lead her to the floor.

That night I learned an important lesson:

Pay attention to t[...] trying to kiss. See[...] low Keith into th[...] to factor in Kati[...] arm's length—[...] a day of stre[...] thing. Second[...] your averag[...] Good vibes[...] nothing. N[...] Keith I [...] envy. If [...] defeat [...] and go[...] But b[...] that [...] was [...] thi[...] ch[...]

"You heard me."

With that, he nodded across the room. Josie was this girl in the other eighth-grade homeroom who had transferred to Hannaford that year from L.A. She has this long brown hair and a sort of big but regal-looking nose. During the World Series she wore a Dodgers cap every day—backward—even though the Dodgers weren't even in it. Definitely a cool thing. She's pretty in a tomboyish sort of a way. Not to mention on the short side.

"What about her?"

"She thinks you're cute."

I blinked. Then sneaked another peak at Josie. She was chatting with Sheila DeCappio, this slightly punked-out girl with a blond streak in her hair. We had written a report together in fourth grade about exotic African mammals.

"Cool it," Derrick said. "Try not to be so obvious."

"How do you know?"

"Easy. She told me."

"Liar. Why'd she tell you?"

"We're friends."

"You're fooling."

"Nope."

"Seriously?"

"Seriously."

I couldn't help myself and glanced again. I noticed her big brown eyes and long lashes. Also, a slight cleft in her chin. Sure, she was pretty flat-chested but I didn't care about that. Lots of girls were still flat.

The problem was that I still had this burning crush on Katie—a girl who obviously couldn't care less if I crawled down a manhole and spent the rest of my life covered in sewage. But here's the weird part: As much as I wanted to give up on her, I simply couldn't. After all, hadn't Katie and I hit it off at Aunt Esther's? Hadn't she said she'd see the show with me? Then held my hand on that short walk into the auditorium!? She had to like me, right? So what was the problem?

Keith, that's what!

If I could get her far away from him, I might stand a chance! At least that's how I figured it. But how could I do that? Yeah, there was an empty room or two upstairs that I knew about. But what were the odds that Katie would go into one of them with me alone? Zero. Still, just as I was mulling it all over, something even weirder happened. Keith was slow dancing with Wendie Culhane, right? Well, suddenly they were making out! Which wouldn't have been so strange except that it was so, I don't know, *public*. I mean, his parents were in the kitchen!

"Check out the stud," Derrick said.

I could tell that he was a little bit envious, too. Who wouldn't be? But before I let my J.Q. send me into a tailspin, I got this idea. Okay, so maybe that beer had gone to my head. Maybe I was just plain desperate. Whatever. At the time it seemed like an inspiration.

Before I could change my mind, I reached for Derrick's beer.

"Gimme that," I said.

"What for?"

"Gimme it!"

I took a long gulp.

"What's up?" Derrick asked.

"I'm gonna ask Katie to slow dance."

Derrick seemed impressed.

"Feeling a good vibe, huh?"

"Damn straight," I lied. "Watch me."

Pretty macho, huh? Before I could change my mind, I marched to Katie's side and asked. She didn't look too thrilled. In fact, she sort of frowned and glanced over her shoulder toward the door. But I guess her good breeding kicked in 'cause she finally shrugged and let me lead her to the floor.

That night I learned an important lesson:

Pay attention to the feelings of a girl you're trying to kiss. See, I was so determined to follow Keith into the land of the lips that I forgot to factor in Katie. For starters, she held me at arm's length—like I had just gotten back from a day of strenuous stall shoveling or something. Second, her body was about as limber as your average department store mannequin. Good vibes? *Not!* I mean, she was giving me nothing. *Nothing!* And when she looked at Keith I thought she was going to cry with envy. If I had been smart I would've accepted defeat like a man, gotten the dance over with, and gone home. Like I said, *if* I had been smart. But by that point I was determined to make that evening turn out the way I wanted if it was the last thing I did on the planet. *The last thing.* So I tried to warm her up with a little chitchat.

"It's good to be with you tonight," I said.

"Uh, yeah," Katie said. "You, too. Thanks for the show."

Yeah, I know. She was too polite to say anything different. But deep down I knew I was in trouble. In so much trouble that I sort of blocked out reality and went into a little fantasy. 'Cause let's face it, fantasy can be a lot more fun sometimes.

I imagined that Katie liked me—and I

mean a lot. Instead of being at Keith's apartment, we were at Tavern on the Green, this fancy restaurant in Central Park. There was a swing band. I was in a tux. Katie had on this long, sexy yellow dress. After a few glasses of champagne I took her to the dance floor, held her really tight, and waltzed her across the room.

"God," she sighed. "You're such a good dancer."

"Thanks," I said suavely. "You, too."

I held her even closer. Our bodies moved perfectly together. I mean, perfectly. The stars shone brightly through the glass ceiling (Tavern on the Green has one of those). As the band segued into "String of Pearls" (my parents' wedding song—one of those romantic oldies), Katie whispered in my ear.

"I love you so much, Matt."

I looked into her blue eyes—eyes as blue as the New York sky on a clear day.

"Oh, Katie," I said. "I love you, too!"

I leaned forward for a kiss.

She smiled . . .

She puckered . . .

I was an inch from her lips!

Half an inch!

But then . . .

She pulled away!

"Matt?" she said sharply. "What're you doing?"

Just like that, she was out of my arms. Suddenly, I wasn't at Tavern on the Green but back in Keith's living room.

"Doing?" I stammered.

"Trying to kiss me?" she spat.

"I was?" I said.

I knew I had been in my fantasy. But had I been so lost there that I'd tried in real life?

Apparently.

"It's getting late," Katie told me. "I should grab a cab."

"A cab?"

"That's right."

"Are you sure you don't want to finish the dance?" I said.

I think she was sure. I mean, she was already heading for the front door.

Seven

People from outside New York City think that if you step onto a sidewalk after dark you'll end up with a knife in your back or something. But the fact is, as long as you stick to well-traveled routes, the city is pretty safe. Even at night. Even for a guy my age. Anyway, on the night of that cast party, if there was anyone in town who could be considered dangerous, that person was me! See, I was mad. Furious. Borderline insane.

You're entitled to know that I had another beer. Now, two beers may not seem like a lot, but to me—a dwarf-loser-lightweight—it was a ton. Like I said, that first beer made me a little bit giddy. Not exactly drunk. Let's just say it had given me the confidence to walk across the room and ask Katie to slow dance.

But that second beer . . . when I first drank it, I didn't feel any different, maybe a little bit looser. But then, it suddenly hit me. *Boom!* I was spinning. Drunk, you might say. Wobbly around the edges. But when you see drunk guys at parties in the movies or on TV, they always seem to be having fun. People that evening might have thought the same about me. After all, I played pool with Derrick. I sang at the piano with Keith's mom. I even danced (not slow) and talked a little bit with Josie! But it was funny. Even though the beers made me *act* happy, they made me *feel* miserable. If anything, the drunkenness intensified my feelings toward Keith. Made them sharper, cleaner. Each time I looked at him kissing Wendie Culhane I remembered how bad the music to *Star Crossed* was. When I overheard him going on about his father's movie I thought of how hard I'd worked to become a good guitar player—I mean, hours and hours of practice!—and how I'd deserved to get that scholarship to Aspen. By the time the party was over and I hit the pavement with Derrick, all my bottled-up feelings—feelings that had been building for most of a year—began to spill out. And I mean *spill*. Then, on the corner of 81st and Columbus Avenue I sort of snapped. I mean, REALLY SNAPPED. All the jealousy, envy, and anger that had been festering in my guts thundered out of me like I was possessed. It was freaky.

"You know what'd make me happy?" I shouted. "If for just once Keith'd suck at every sport!"

Poor Derrick. He looked sort of stunned. Don't forget, he didn't know me that well. He had thought Keith was my best pal. That I loved him. Which he was and I did. But . . .

"You know what else? I'd love it if every girl in the city hated him!"

A man walking his poodle shot me a look and jogged by.

"Every girl?" Derrick said.

"Right!" I said.

"Whoa . . . that's pretty harsh."

"So what?" I said, pacing. "He deserves it. You know what he said tonight?"

"What?"

"That *Star Crossed* was good enough for Broadway!"

"Really?"

"Damn straight! And didn't you hear how he was bragging about Sandra Millicent?"

"Not really . . ."

"Well, he was!"

I jumped up and slapped the awning of a building on 81st Street.

"Sandra Millicent," I said. "What's so great about her?"

I slapped that awning again. Harder this time.

"Have you looked at her up close?"

"Close?" Derrick said.

I wheeled around and faced him.

"At Sandra Millicent! I mean, the woman looks like a . . . a horse!"

Wouldn't you know it? Right on the word "horse," my voice cracked! Again! But I was so pissed I wasn't even embarrassed. And Derrick? I guess I had finally gone too far. He shook his head and grinned.

"That is deep-down weird," he said. "A horse? No way."

I suppose Derrick was right. Sandra Millicent is one of the most gorgeous women in the world. There's nothing remotely horsey about her. No long nose, no mane. Still, I didn't care. My father says that venting your emotions from time to time can be healthy. Well, that's how it made me feel right then. A little guilty, yeah. But cleansed, if you know what I mean. Beautifully purified of all the junk I'd been lugging around on my back. I leaned against a parked car. It was strange, but I felt sort of peaceful all of a sudden.

If the evening had ended right then I think

I might've gone home, gone to sleep, and woken up the next day a new man. The trouble was I suddenly got this strong feeling that I was being watched. In fact, I was sure of it. I wheeled around and bingo! There was this guy staring at me. He was a fairly typical street person—middle-aged, glassy-eyed, a beard. At first, I felt sort of relieved that it wasn't somebody I knew. I mean, can you imagine? But then it turned out to be almost worse. Because this man suddenly smiled at me really big, exposing a line of uneven, but surprisingly white teeth.

"Better be careful," he said. He had this deep voice that seemed to rumble out of him. "Wishes that strong can come true."

With that, he stumbled off into the night.

For a moment Derrick and I were stone silent. A bus passed, but aside from that the street was dead. We exchanged a quick glance. I grinned. He grinned back. The whole thing seemed so crazy. Next thing I knew, we were laughing like two seventh-grade girls. Our voices echoed among the buildings like we were in the Grand Canyon.

"Wild," Derrick said.

"Yeah," I agreed.

"That dude is from another planet."

"Uh-huh."

"Wishes can't come true," Derrick said.

We paused, then started laughing all over again.

"Hey, man," I said finally. "Sorry about the yelling."

Derrick waved a hand.

"No problem. We've all got to let loose now and then."

All in all, Derrick was pretty nice about the whole thing. Make that *really* nice.

Just then, the crosstown pulled up. Wouldn't you know it? It was one of the ones with Keith's million-dollar gums on the side. Yeah, I felt this brief irritation jolt—but I did my best to put it out of my mind. Last thing I needed was to throw another fit, right? Besides, I had to get home.

"Come on!" I said.

Derrick and I ran across 81st Street and jumped on.

"Hey, Matt," he said as we took seats in the back.

"Yeah?"

"Don't get too down. Remember what I said about Josie."

I smiled. No doubt about it. Definitely more than a sometimes friend. Who cared if he had red dreads and lived in a closet?

"I'll remember," I said.

The crosstown bus is actually pretty fast.

A few moments later we were through the park and at Madison Avenue: Derrick's stop.

"Speak to you later?" he said.

We slapped five.

"You got it!"

With that, he got off and I rode farther east to Second Avenue. Back home, I collapsed straight into my bed. Which is when I found out something else. A couple of beers can really knock a guy out. I slept like a log.

Eight

*B*rrrriinnnggg!
Brrrrinnnnnnnngggggggg!!

Though the nearest phone is in our front hallway, it sounded like the ring mechanism had been surgically implanted in my brain. Talk about loud. Then again, if I hadn't had those beers maybe my head wouldn't have been splitting. Okay, so maybe not *splitting*. More like a low, dull ache. But it made me feel sort of grown up to imagine I had this killer hangover.

Anyway, I opened one eye and peeked at the clock: 9:30. Ugh! Who would call at 9:30? And on a Saturday? No one *I* knew. Probably some card pal of my mom's wanting to arrange a poker date. Or else my sister from school to ask for more cash. She did that quite a bit—though she usually had the good sense to wait until at least eleven. No way it was for me. Keith knew how I liked to sleep in.

I fluffed up my pillow a bit and closed my eyes.

"Matt! . . . Matt!"

My mom. Seconds later I heard the sound of her clogs hitting the wood floor, coming toward my room.

"Phone call, honey."

"Can you take a message?" I begged, eyes still closed.

"Well, I suppose." Then there was this weird pause. "I'll ask *her*."

Her? *Her??* Did I have my pronouns right? Or was I more hungover than I thought?

"It's a *girl?*" I asked.

"Hmmm," Mom said. You could tell she was enjoying this.

Just like that, my heart starting pumping about twenty gallons a second. Because suddenly I knew beyond a shadow of a doubt who it was: Katie Robinson, calling to beg my forgiveness.

"Oh, Matt," she'd cry. "I was such an idiot. Keith is nice and all, but . . . well, don't take this the wrong way . . . I know he's your best friend—but don't you think he's sort of shallow? I mean, what's he trying to prove with that hair? And that sixties outfit? Ohmigawd. Can you say *pathetic?*"

After that, she'd invite me over for brunch—and greet me at her front door wearing nothing but a pair of argyle kneesocks and a thong.

"Come on, Matt," Mom said, sort of irritated now.

I'm always amazed at how little time it can take to jump into a pretty detailed fantasy. Or how quick a person can come to believe his thoughts—no matter how crazy. I mean, maybe she wouldn't be wearing a thong but by that point I was certain that it'd be Katie on the phone. So sure that I roused myself from bed and marched past my mom (grinning like a maniac) straight to the front hallway. On the way, I caught my reflection in this antique mirror we have. Talk about gruesome! My hair was sticking out in about ten thousand and three directions. Not to mention that I was in my underwear and a ripped *Spider-Man* T-shirt. Thank God, Katie couldn't see me. But I knew she'd be able to hear me. Which was a problem, as I'm quite prone to early morning crackage. And since I wasn't too psyched about a possible repeat performance of the "Matt Greene, boy soprano" routine, I took a second to clear my throat. Only then did I reach for that phone.

"Hello?" I said.

Yes!!! This time the old vocal chords registered low and gravelly—sort of like one of those private eyes in the old movies who sleep in their clothes and gargle each morning with a tumbler of scotch.

"Hi . . . Matt?"

Well, I was so pumped by my low, mellow tones that I was all primed to plow ahead with a "Hi, Katie." But I stopped myself. That's because I suddenly realized that the "she" on the other end of the line didn't sound like the "she" I'd imagined. The voice sounded a little bit lower, huskier. So I decided to get a little more info.

"Yeah," I said. "It's Matt. Uh, who is this, please?"

"Josie," the voice said. "You know . . . from school . . ."

A wave of gooseflesh ripped across my body. *Josie!?* Lemme tell you, I was floored, shot between the eyes with the phaser set to stun. Josie was the last person I'd figured I'd hear from. I mean, I knew what Derrick had told me. But with my self-confidence registering in negative numbers, I didn't completely believe him. Okay, Josie and I had danced a little bit at Keith's party. Even chitchatted. Pretty easily, too. But not "I'll call you tomorrow" easily. More like, "See you at school Monday and maybe we'll nod at each other in the hall."

"Josie?" I said.

"Yes," she replied. "We talked last night. Am I calling too early?"

"No, no," I said. "I was hanging around my room, practicing guitar."

I don't know why I said that. Because last I heard, lying in bed unconscious wasn't the best way to improve your fingering. But I'm still glad I came up with that little lie 'cause suddenly Josie seemed more relaxed. Which made me more relaxed. In fact, I think we may have gotten into a decent conversational groove right then if my dad hadn't decided that this was the precise moment he needed to get the morning *Times*. And do you think he did it quickly? You know, opened the front door, picked up the paper, and got out of my space? Nah, that would've been too nice. Instead, he walked by—no, make that *strolled*—real slow, and when he passed, he raised his eyebrows and grinned even bigger than Mom had by my bedroom door. It's amazing how parents go ape when their kids start to date. I mean, is my mom and dad's love life so stale that they have to live it through a loser like me? It's sort of sad when you think about it.

Anyway, Dad's little look got me so distracted that I missed what Josie said next. And when I said, "Sorry, what was that?" it threw her off big-time. I mean, she began to stutter. Seriously. In a way I felt bad. But also sort of good. It was kind of neat to think that *I* was making someone that nervous. But who knew? Maybe *her* dad had just walked by and thrown off *her* timing, too. Maybe she was sitting in the middle of her living room with her entire extended family gathered around in a circle. Maybe a great-aunt about 110 was asking her to speak directly into her hearing aid while a stenographer took notes.

"I'm sorry," I said, after Josie stammered around for a couple of seconds. "My dad just walked by."

"Oh, that's all right," Josie said with a nervous giggle. That seemed to calm her down. "I was just saying that last night was fun."

"Yeah," I said. "Fun."

Great comeback, huh? But what do you want? Two minutes earlier I had been sound asleep, right?

"So . . . did you like the musical?"

Sure, I knew that she was just trying to make conversation. I mean, how could Josie have known that asking me if I thought *Star Crossed* was any good was the equivalent of asking Davy Crockett if he had enjoyed his stay at the Alamo? My J.Q. went from zero to sixty in about half a millisecond. Still, I was careful not to pitch another fit. Yeah, I was a little groggy—but I wasn't a complete moron. After all, a girl had called me at home—no everyday occurrence! If I blew this, I would be the New Jersey Nets of dating. The biggest loser in New York City history. No, I had to play this one just right.

"Yeah," I said. "The show was tremendous."

That's the word I used: "tremendous." Can you believe that?

"Yeah," Josie said. "Keith did a good job."

"Oh, yes," I said. "Tremendous."

"But . . ."

But? Had Josie used the word "but"? My heart filled with hope.

"But what?" I said, maybe a bit too eagerly.

"Well," Josie said. "I feel bad saying this 'cause I know what good friends you guys are. I liked a lot of the lyrics and the cast was great but . . ."

Again with the "but"!

"Yeah?" I was dying. "But what?"

"But don't you think the music . . . well, that it sort of stunk?"

The music stunk?!

Music to my ears!

"Like I said," Josie went on quickly. "I feel bad saying that."

"No, no," I said. "I actually agree." Then I couldn't resist. "You know Keith only knows four chords on the guitar."

"Really?"

"Really."

"Gosh," she said. "No wonder."

There was a little pause then—sort of like we had agreed on something important. I don't know what Josie was thinking but I know what *I* was: that if I blew this now I would have to either a) throw myself in front of a rapidly moving vehicle, such as a cab or subway; or b) throw myself in front of a slowly moving but extremely heavy vehicle, such as an industrial-sized rototiller or steamroller.

Anyway, that's when Josie got around to the point of the call.

"Listen," she said finally. She suddenly sounded nervous again. "The reason I was calling . . ."

"Yeah?"

"Well, you know the basketball game next Friday?"

71

Of course I knew. Hannaford was playing Trinity for the seventh-and-eighth-grade private school championship. Guess who was the star of our team? You got it: Keith.

"Sure," I said.

"Oh, good," Josie said. "Well, see, I was wondering if you were going?" Then she added quickly, "I mean . . . if you wanted to go together?"

Go together??

It was all I could do to not break into a Sioux victory dance (we studied the Sioux back in fifth grade). I mean, this was one for the record books! Me! Little Matt Greene. *Asked out by a girl!* And a nice girl, too. A girl, as it turned out, with excellent taste in musicals. Sure, she wasn't someone I had given two seconds' thought to before Keith's party. But a lot can happen in a night, right? Dictatorships can fall. Planets can collide. And girls like Katie Robinson can ignore a guy to the point where he feels like a refugee from one of those third-world countries whose gross national product is about three dollars. But just like that, that *same* guy can find himself becoming attracted to a new girl—a girl with a penchant for Dodgers caps. A girl with a cute little cleft in her chin. A girl with no tits. But who really cared about that? Hey, I didn't shave yet, right? The way I saw it, we were more than even.

Anyway, before I said yes, I stunned myself. I really did. I didn't know I had it in me to be so smooth.

"The game sounds wonderful," I said. "And maybe we could grab some dinner beforehand?"

Boy, did that ever take Josie by surprise.

"Sure," she said. "Yeah . . . that would be great."

"Do you like Chinese food?"

"Absolutely."

"There's an Empire Szechuan about three blocks from school."

"I know that one," she said.

"Good enough."

"Great, then. I'm psyched."

"So am I," I said. "Should be cool."

"Yeah, awesome."

Anyway, it went on like that until somewhere along the line we both ran short on adjectives. Which is when the conversation began to lag. With the date arranged what else was there to say? After chatting about school a bit we wrapped things up pretty quickly. And when I hung up the phone? Well, I felt as good as . . . well, as good as I'd felt since I had made that date with Katie a week earlier. In other words, like the king of the world!

Yes!!!!

Now . . . if I could only get back to my room before the parental units grabbed me for the post–phone call debriefing . . .

No such luck. Because as it turned out, Mom and Dad had settled in with the newspaper at the glass breakfast table in the corner of our living room. And lemme tell you: The very second I put down the phone, whatever articles they were eyeballing got dull in a hurry. I didn't take more than a half a step toward my room before Mom began the cross-examination.

"Was that Katie?" she asked.

Talk about getting right to the point! Was I sorry that I'd confided in her about that date. But since I'd already dug myself into a hole, I had to answer.

"Actually, no."

Mom shot Dad a glance.

"No?" she said, all concerned. "What happened to Katie, then?"

There was only one way to handle this line of questioning. Keep the answers short and vague.

"Well," I said. "I'm not really sure . . ."

With that crumb, I took another step

toward my room. But Dad stopped me dead.

"Not sure?" he asked.

That's when I sighed. I was sunk. Why fight the inevitable? They were going to get it out of me eventually. Suddenly, it seemed silly not to tell them and get it over with.

"To tell the truth," I said, "Katie liked Keith."

Boy, you should've seen the way Mom took *that* news. Her eyes went real wide. Then her whole face seemed to cave in on itself. She looked flat-out crushed. Mothers can look that way sometimes.

"Oh, I'm sorry, honey."

You'd have thought I had told her I needed a new liver. But then she saw an opportunity to cheer me up.

"But now this new girl is calling?"

"Yeah," I managed. "Josie."

"Is she nice?"

Is she *nice?* What kind of a question was that? I wanted out of there so badly I thought of shocking my parents into shutting up by saying something like, "*Nice* in the sack, anyway . . . or so says the high school football team. . . ."

Trouble is, my dad's heard it all from his patients. He'd probably giggle like a madman and start taking notes if I said something racy like that. Besides, I didn't have the guts. So I fell back to the old standby: short and vague.

"Nice enough," I said.

"And now you're going out with her?" Mom asked.

"Yeah. To the basketball game next Friday."

That seemed to satisfy her big-time. Another enormous grin spread over her face—the kind you see on the faces of those religious converts who hand out flyers in bus stations. God, parents can be so easy to please sometimes. Even though he was more laid-back about it, you could tell that Dad was pumped too.

"That's life sometimes," he said. "You think you want one thing but when that doesn't work out, something else comes your way."

A life lesson. I guess they're part of his job description. By that point I'm sure I was blushing. Not to mention desperate for an escape. So when my mom told me to get dressed before breakfast, I don't have to tell you how fast I moved my butt out of there—somewhere between warp 8 and light speed.

Nine

I know what you're probably thinking—that I spent the week leading up to the big date with Josie floating on a cloud or whatever it is that people float on when they're psyched about something—especially if that something is a girl. I'll bet you're thinking that I thought about Josie morning, noon, and night. That I imagined things like whisking her off to the art supply closet after school to lick her neck and smear her body with finger paint.

You'd be wrong. Instead of thinking exciting things like that, I spent most of the week slowly torturing myself. And by torture I mean *torture*. See, I had hoped that ranting like a maniac on the corner of 81st and Columbus after Keith's party had purged me of my jealousy. Well, let's just say I had work to do. Because the minute I was done with breakfast on Saturday morning, who should call?

Keith.

And, boy, did he ever have news.

Horrifying, J.Q.–elevating news!

He had gotten to third base with Wendie Culhane!

As in below the belt! As in . . . well, *you know.* And with a *tenth grader!* Talk about serious! At first I didn't believe him. But when Keith described the scene to me—how later that night he had taken her upstairs to his room, how they had begun to make out, how she had asked him to take off his shirt . . . well, it was enough to make a guy sick. But what made me even sicker was the I'm-the-King-of-the-World, full-of-it way Keith told me. You'd have thought he had come up with a cure for mad cow disease. Of course, in retrospect, I realize that Keith wasn't really behaving all *that* badly. That in a way he was actually fairly restrained. I admit it: If I had gotten to third with a girl like Wendie Culhane, I probably would've phoned *The New York Times* and demanded space on page one. So maybe Keith wasn't all *that* terrible. Just excited. And, to tell the truth, the side of me that was his best friend wanted him to enjoy it. With the success of *Star Crossed,* he had a right to his happiness.

The trouble was that for the rest of the weekend, I couldn't get *his happiness* off my mind. It rattled through my brain over and over and over again like a mantra from a place where sexually immature eighth graders go to die: "Keith got to third with Wendie Culhane! Keith got to third with Wendie Culhane! Keith got to third with . . ."

The next afternoon, my grandmother visited. Lemme tell you: It's close to impossible to carry on a conversation with your nana when you're imagining your best friend sticking his hands down a tenth grader's pants.

But what was really bad about it is that somewhere along the line, Keith's success sort of devalued Josie in my eyes. I mean, who was she? An eighth grader? With no breasts! How could she compare with a high school sex goddess like Wendie?

But there was this even bigger problem. Now that Josie and I had planned our big date we didn't quite know how to behave in front of each other. Take that Monday. I found her at lunch and tried to get a little chitchat going.

"Hey," I said. "What's up?"

"Not much," Josie said. "You?"

"Not much."

(Awkward moment of a mind-numbing nature.)

"Got history today?" I said.

"Yeah."

"Yeah? Me, too."

"Oh . . ."

(Second awkward moment of a mind-numbing nature.)

"Well," I said. "I've got to find Keith."

"Okay . . . bye."

"Bye," I said. "Enjoy your salad."

Enjoy your salad? What was I thinking? That I was chatting up a rabbit? Anyway, I'll spare you the other times I tried to break the ice. Let's just say that Josie and I were like one of those floes you see in documentaries about the Arctic—unbreakable. By the end of the week I was praying she'd cancel. I mean, how could we possibly get through dinner? We had nothing—and I mean *nothing*—to say to each other. Unless the waiter decided to join us, we were dead.

With Keith basking in the glow of his extra base hit, I felt a little funny confiding in him about something so trivial. So late that Friday afternoon, with the date a few short hours away, I cornered my new buddy, Derrick, in the school courtyard.

"Relax," he said. "I know exactly what you should do."

"You do?"

"Sure. You got a pen?"

Next thing I knew I was writing a list of things to say to Josie on my forearms with a ballpoint. That way, Derrick explained, if I got stuck for something to say, I could casually roll up my sleeves and get some quick inspiration. Here's some of what I wrote (mostly Derrick's suggestions):

Do you like Mr. Freyer? (English teacher)
You look beautiful this evening.
Doesn't school lunch suck?
Your hair smells exquisite.
Are you a fan of the classical guitar?
Where did you go to school before
Hannaford? Was it fun?
How lucky you are to have such a prominent cleft in your chin.

Yeah, I know . . . but the way I viewed it, I'd be lucky to get out of the evening alive. I fully expected a disaster. Which makes me feel S-T-U-P-I-D stupid about how things really went. I don't know who said it first but I'll say it now: Life is weird. Way weird. Because after raking myself over the coals for a solid week, what do you think happened? Josie and I HIT IT OFF!

Sure, there were some rocky moments at the beginning. She looked so cute when I picked her up (blue jean skirt, white top, yellow sandals) that I could barely form words. Then on the walk over to the Chinese place, when I could finally throw together some sentences, the conversation was pretty forced. Worse, when I told her, "Your hair smells exquisite," she thought I said, "Your hair smells, what is it?" and got a little bit hurt. Basically, it wasn't until I downshifted to more basic questions like, "When did you become a Dodgers fan?" that the conversation finally began to roll. And then it was pure magic. I swear that by the time we were seated in the Empire Szechuan, global warming had kicked in and that rock-solid Arctic ice had turned to slush. We must've felt uptight at school, because the waiter didn't have to join us to keep things going. I didn't have to look at the fifteen or so other questions and compliments I had scribbled up my arms. Instead, the conversation took on a life of its own. After baseball we debated the pros and cons of dodgeball versus Capture the Flag. We chatted about our favorite flicks. Then about her dad who still lived in L.A. and grew up on a dairy farm but was now a sound technician for TV shows. Then her mom who used to be a rock drummer but who moved to New York to work for a literary agency. Then about my sister, who as far as I could tell wanted to spend her life locked in her room, even at boarding school, listening to show tunes. Anyway, we talked.

Even better, we laughed.

First, when I accidentally dipped my sleeve in the duck sauce. But then at everything. At people in our class. Teachers. Ms. Finkle. The guy sitting two tables over trying to impress his date by talking about his stock portfolio. Even our waiter's shoes (penny loafers with red socks). We laughed so often and so easily that by the end of the meal I felt I was in love. It's crazy, I know. But the thing is, it's true. I'll tell you something: I even had this little fantasy about playing shortstop for the Yankees and Josie announcing the game play-by-play for NBC, then about getting married in center field of Yankee Stadium during a doubleheader. And me hitting a homer and dedicating it to her in the postgame show. Weird, huh? But I was having that much fun. Besides, I could think of worse places to get married. And worse people to be married to.

So you might say the date was going well. But just around the time the meal was over, what was going "well" suddenly got bizarre. See, Josie and I started chatting about song lyrics—Beatles, mostly. (She knows "I Am the Walrus" by heart! Yes!!!!!!) Anyway, after gabbing about John, Paul, George, and Ringo for a few minutes, Josie let spill that she sometimes jotted down little nonsensical poems. Don't ask me why but all of a sudden I had to hear one—just *had* to. In fact, I became somewhat of a pain in the butt about it, if you want to know the truth. I wouldn't shut up until she told me one. Of course, she said all the things somebody says when they're put on the spot like that. Things like, "Oh, they're just little things I whipped off." And, "They really suck. I can't!" But I kept at her and wore her down. Finally, she blushed a little, looked both ways to make sure no one was listening, then leaned forward.

"Well, I guess I can tell you one of them. It's called 'Cyrus Henry Merkle.'"

"'Cyrus Henry Merkle'?" I asked. "Who's he?"

"Just some guy I made up."

"Okay. Go for it."

I was psyched. I really was. With that, Josie looked around again. But then, she frowned.

"Maybe I shouldn't," she said. "It's so dumb."

"So what?" I said. "I love dumb."

"You sure?"

"Sure I'm sure. Please."

"Really?"

"*Really!*"

To cut to the chase, she made about a hundred more excuses but finally spat it out:

> *"Cyrus Henry Merkle*
> *Lived at the Arctic Circle*
> *In a frozen paradise*
> *Farming fields of ice.*
>
> *Said Merkle to a seal*
> *On the spacious Arctic shelf:*
> *'I've got ninety miles of ice*
> *And I growed it all meself!'"*

Now I know that taken out of context this may not seem all that funny. You might even say it's stupid. Dumb, as Josie put it. Which, let's face it, in a way, it is. But before you judge it, you've got to know that Josie said the final two lines, "I've got ninety miles of ice/And I growed it all meself!" with this really thick British accent. I think it was the accent that got me.

Sure, the poem was dumb. But it was so *perfectly* dumb. So brilliantly stupid that I had to grin. And the more I thought about little Cyrus Henry Merkle farming his ice shelf, the more I had to giggle. Next thing I knew, Josie started in too. Then she was laughing. And then *I* was laughing. And pretty soon the laughing built so that we were really shaking. It's like all the tension we had been feeling all the week of the date fell away in an instant. I mean, we were suddenly hysterical. To the point where people started to look. To the point where I was worried that moo shu pork was going to stream out of my nose. I almost had to get up and collect myself. In fact, Josie *did* stand up and turn away so she wouldn't look at me. But when she sat back down we started up again—not quite so bad, but still bad enough. And then, when we finally began to get hold of ourselves, the waiter with the red socks and penny loafers asked us if everything was all right and we lost it all over again! We were truly out of control! In fact, I think I'd still be laughing at that dumb poem if I hadn't happened to glance toward the window of the restaurant. Because that's when the evening began to get really bizarre. You'll never guess who I saw there:

Wendie Culhane!

Now I know that, taken by itself, simply seeing Wendie Culhane isn't bizarre at all. But when you add who she was with, well . . . Wendie wasn't with Keith. Not by a long shot. Instead, she was with a girl—a pretty girl, in fact, with auburn hair and big green eyes. Not only that, a girl who suddenly gave Wendie a playful little shove up against the glass window of the restaurant. And then leaned forward . . .

And planted one square on Wendie's lips!!!!

No peck, either! We're talking a real kiss—at least five—no, make that ten, seconds! And something told me that Keith didn't know a thing about the two of them. I mean, that morning in homeroom he had gone off about how Wendie's parents were going away for the weekend soon. How he and she would be spending the night in her parents' very own bed! Well, from what I saw, Keith was in for one megadeath surprise. Yeah, he had gotten to third with Wendie. But the way I saw it, she had already switched teams.

I guess my shock must've been plastered all over my face. Just as Wendie and the mystery lady were breaking the clinch and heading arm in arm down the street, Josie, still a bit giggly, glanced over her shoulder toward the window.

"What's going on?" she asked.

"Going on?" I stammered. "Nothing . . . just someone I know with someone I don't know."

Josie must have sensed from my tone she should let it drop. Besides, right then, the waiter laid this check down next to me. He was probably trying to get rid of us before we got laughing again and forced him to call the riot squad. Josie reached for her wallet. But my sister had taught me a thing or two about dating.

"No, no," I said casually. "I've got it."

Boy, did Josie look pleased. "Really?"

"Sure," I said. "My treat."

Josie smiled wide. "All right," she said. But then she added something. . . .

Are you ready?

"But the next time's on me, okay?"

Which was all I needed to knock Wendie Culhane and the mystery girl clear out of my head—at least for the time being. I mean, did you hear what Josie said?

"But the next time's on me, okay?"

As in, there would be one. You know, a *next time.*

Ten

Like most Manhattan types, my folks are pretty liberal-minded. And I suppose that sort of "live and let live" thinking has rubbed off on my sister and me. Even so, as Josie and I were walking to school for the big game, I've got to admit that I had started to feel pretty darned pleased with how I was handling the whole "Wendie Culhane could be a lesbo" situation. I was trying hard not to judge it. The way I figured it, Wendie Culhane could do what she wanted with whoever she wanted. Hey, she could kiss a female gopher, for all I cared. Just as long as it didn't hurt anyone—and no one contracted rabies.

Anyway, even though I was taking the high road with Wendie, it wasn't long before I started to worry about what in the world I could say to Keith about it. I mean, what was the protocol? Flat out tell him that his girl-friend wished he had breasts? Would it soften the blow to tell him that the girl was cute?

Well, as you can imagine, with thoughts like these I was pretty stressed by the time Josie and I reached school. Luckily, the packed gym was just what I needed to get my mind off the subject. Derrick was sitting with some other guys about ten rows up. I could spot his red dreadlocks anywhere. Ms. Finkle was courtside with her husband, this surprisingly studly looking guy, and their two little kids.

It took Josie and me about five minutes to fight our way to the bleachers and another five to climb to the top for seats. And the second we got settled a bunch of Trinity rooters took off on their school cheer. So of course we Hannafordites felt obligated to answer with ours. Soon I was so busy cheering that Wendie Culhane became a distant memory. Finally, the buzzer sounded and the starters took their positions at midcourt. Keith led the way, his hair tied back in a ponytail.

"Isn't this the coolest?" Josie said. "The championship game!"

She did look excited! The more time I spent with her the more I liked her. I mean, you had to like a girl who could get pumped about basketball, right? Right. And just like that, another buzzer sounded. The gym got real quiet . . . the two centers stood opposite each other . . . the ref dribbled a few times . . . and tossed up the opening jump ball . . .

Game time!

Lemme tell you, it was a real old-fashioned, gut-wrenching, scream-like-a-maniac squeaker. First they went up. Then we went up. Then them. Then us. Then them. Then us. Until suddenly we were down by one with ten seconds to play. I was hoarse from shouting. So was Josie. So was everybody.

After a time-out the buzzer sounded and both teams returned to the floor with the game on the line. It was our ball.

Now usually there'd be no question about what would happen next. We'd lie back and wait for Keith to save the day. I mean, he averaged about twenty-five points a game and ten boards. But for practically the first time in his entire life, Keith was having a so-so game. Not terrible. But not great, either. Yeah, he had scored fifteen points. But he had done it on about twenty million shots. And some of those were real doozies. In the second quarter, he launched a three pointer that ended up in Mr. Finkle's lap. And in the third, he went for a hook shot that was so off it turned into a pass to Trinity's center which led to a fast break. As a sportscaster would say, Keith wasn't "feeling it." As the two eleventh-grade jerks sitting behind Josie and me did say: "He's blowing donkey chunks."

Anyway, as the team took the court for the final play, the cheers and clapping and bleacher stamping all blended together into this really intense, really horrible, really beautiful noise. Beautiful not because it sounded good. But because it was pumped full of just about every emotion you could possibly think of. All in all, I'd say that the Hannaford gym was as noisy as your average rocket launch.

That is, until the ref blew the whistle again. 'Cause just like that, the place got real quiet. Not bored quiet. Edge-of-your-seat quiet. Then all of a sudden *boom!*—the ball was in play! Scotty Parker, our guard, dribbled up-court as the four other Hannaford players, Keith included, ran ahead of him to get in position. Now, I was psyched in 2000 when there was a Subway Series between the Mets and Yankees. But with the pros you're always a little bit distanced from the event. I mean, Mike Piazza is a great catcher and seems like a good guy in interviews. But, let's face it, if I passed him on the street he'd walk right by. Probably on his way to take $20 million out of the bank to buy himself a new Mercedes or a small Caribbean island. Same with any other pro. Those guys are too rich to relate to. But this game—this little seventh-and-eighth-grade championship—was in my own school. I mean, I *knew* these players. One was my best friend even! The pride of Hannaford was on the line! I was pumped. Psyched!

"Come on, Scotty!" Josie yelled as the guard brought the ball across midcourt.

I glanced at the clock.

Only six seconds left!

"You can do it!" Josie cried again.

Now five!

"Do something, moron!" one of the jerks behind me called.

I have to admit I agreed. If Scotty wasn't careful, he'd run out the clock!

"Make a move!" I shrieked.

I don't kid myself that I had anything to do with it, but that's the exact moment Scotty pulled off this little stutter step and broke left . . . then back right . . . then left again . . .

Toward the basket!

They weren't going to Keith after all! Scotty was taking it to the hole by himself!

But wait!

Just then, the Trinity defense collapsed around Scotty. Keith cut sharp. Scotty dished him the ball underhand. Keith had a clear layup!

Yes!

But no!

The Trinity center grabbed his arms and pulled him to the floor.

The whistle blew.

"Foul!" the ref called.

The gym went nuts. I looked at the clock: .5 seconds left in the game! Now it was simple: Keith had two foul shots. If he made one we'd go to overtime. If he made both—Hannaford would win!

"He'll do it," I told Josie. "Keith's great from the line."

It was true. Keith hit an average of about eighty percent. I mean, some pros don't even shoot that well from the stripe. So, overtime was a lock. And victory? Pretty damned likely. We Hannaford fans were certain of it. The Trinity people too. Because even though they started waving their arms and chanting, "MISS THAT SHOT! MISS THAT SHOT!" as Keith walked to the free-throw line, they looked sort of depressed. Which under the circumstances was completely understandable.

Keith took a few dribbles . . . looked toward the basket . . . found his range . . . lifted the ball over his head . . .

And clanged the first shot off the rim!

Boy, did that ever give the Trinity geeks a whiff of oxygen! "MISS THAT SHOT!" got about ten billion times louder. We Hannafordites answered with, "You can do it, Keith!" "Come on, Keith!" "No biggie, Keith!" and any other encouraging thing that popped into our heads. If Keith sunk the next one, we went to overtime. If he missed . . . well, he couldn't miss, right? I mean, we were talking about Keith Livingston.

The ref tossed the ball back to the man of the minute. As the gym rocked and the bleachers shook, Keith stood there in the eye of the storm, dribbling slowly, almost like he was bored or something—like he was playing some meaningless pickup game in the park. His miss hadn't shaken his confidence one bit. When he was done, he took what seemed like three minutes to wipe some sweat off his brow and adjust the tie thingee on his ponytail. Only then did he look up at the hoop and get ready for that final shot. Boy, was he cool! A guy that cool had to come through. I mean, it was a lock. I just knew it.

Turned out I didn't know much. 'Cause that's when something downright, grab-your-jockstrap bizarre happened. Yep, Keith missed. But that's not the half of it. Right there in the

Hannaford gym—on his own home court, with hundreds of people watching—Keith Livingston, the coolest cucumber in the grade, the kid so good-looking he'd been immortalized on crosstown buses the whole city wide . . .

Tossed up an air ball!

That's right: an *AIR BALL!!!!!!!!!*

The buzzer sounded! While the Trinity fans stormed the court like a herd of under-exercised broncos, we Hannafordites sat stone quiet, too stunned to move.

I know what you're thinking: that after the success of *Star Crossed* and Keith's track record with the babes, I was secretly happy to see my friend brought down a notch or two. But I felt bad for him. Writing a musical was one thing. But blowing the school championship? With an *air ball?* That is on a whole other plane. I felt for the guy. I mean, *ouch!* And you should have seen him, too. He walked sort of dazed through the sea of Trinity fans and crumpled up on the bench. Then he undid his ponytail so his blond locks fell down on either side of his head like a pair of yellow curtains. He hid his face in his hands. Seconds later, the coach, Mr. Phillips, leaned over and patted his shoulder. And it looked like Scotty Parker tried to say something nice. But everyone else? They treated him like he had an extremely contagious strain of leprosy. If ever a picture shouted "I need a friend," this was it.

Trouble was, the Trinity kids had taken over the court and were whooping it up big-time. Some were doing cartwheels. Others were singing that stupid school song of theirs again. One guy was jumping up and down, waving his arms like a windmill, shouting, "Trinity rules! Trinity rules!" I don't need to tell you that the last thing I wanted to do was fight my way through that! But since it was the only route to Keith, I didn't have much choice.

"You wanna?" I said to Josie.

She nodded, sort of grimly. "I guess."

But before I could make my move toward Keith, I felt this tap on my arm: Derrick.

"Hey, Matt," he said, then nodded to Josie. "Mind if I steal him from you for two seconds?"

Josie looked surprised. "Be my guest."

Before I knew it, Derrick was pulling me aside.

"How're the questions working?" he asked.

I glanced at my forearms. It seemed like ages since I had covered them with ink.

"I didn't need them," I said. "It's going great."

Derrick smiled. "Cool, man."

"Thanks for your help, though."

"No problem."

"Listen," I said. "Is that all? Because I want to . . ."

I nodded at Josie. Derrick smiled.

"Sure," he said. "Three's a crowd. Catch you later."

As I watched Derrick cut away from me, I couldn't help remembering the night we had become friends: at Keith's cast party. And that led me to thinking about those idiotic wishes I had made afterward on the corner of 81st and Columbus. Which is when this major-league chill ran through me. I looked toward my buddy, still on the bench with his head in his hands. Had *I* caused it? After all, I *had* said that I wished he would screw up in sports. And also that his love life would go down the toilet—which would explain Wendie Culhane and her new friend. For a fraction of a second the thought of it all made me sort of panicky. But only for a fraction. I mean, I was too much my dad's son to really fall for that kind of junk. Wishes don't come true. Keith screwed up because he screwed up. Wendie made out with a girl 'cause, well, who knew why. But it sure had nothing to do with me. *Nothing.* I turned back to Josie.

"Come on," I said. "Let's check Keith out."

Once we got going, it didn't take long for

us to weave our way around the Trinity fans. One thing was certain: Regardless of who caused my buddy to miss those shots, it was sure tough to see how hard he was taking it. He still hadn't looked up. Not even when Josie and I stood right in front of him.

"Hey," I said, finally.

Nothing. I glanced at Josie, then back at my friend.

"Keith," I said. "It's me."

He finally raised his head. His eyes were red. As in tears. I felt terrible.

"Hey," he said, weakly. "Hey, Josie."

We said hi and then this silence settled over us. You'd have thought someone's dog had died. But I had to say something.

"Just remember. We never would have gotten this far without you."

That got me a shrug.

"Everybody has bad games," I went on. "You're still the best athlete in the class."

With another shrug he buried his head in his hands again. Maybe Keith just wanted to be left alone? Besides, out of the corner of my eye, I saw his mom, dad, and little sis waiting for me to finish up. But as I was about to turn away:

"Hey," he said, and motioned me to come closer.

I kneeled in front of him. He rubbed his eyes and looked searchingly around the gym, then back at me.

"During the second quarter . . . I noticed that Wendie wasn't here."

I drew in a sharp breath.

"Wendie?" I squeaked.

"It ate at me all game." Keith scowled. "Ah, what the hell. *Girls!*"

I couldn't believe it. So that's why he screwed up! He was stewing about Wendie! I thought that Keith had had so many girl-friends he didn't care about any one in partic-ular. Love 'em and leave 'em. But maybe he had finally met his match?

"Ah, whatever," Keith said. Then, before I knew it, he leaned forward and gave me this massive hug.

"Thanks for coming over to talk to the out-cast."

"No problem."

Keith pulled away. "See you tomorrow morning."

"Tomorrow?" I said. "Where?"

Keith frowned. "At Nick's, fool!"

For the past year or so, Keith and I had been meeting every other Saturday morning for breakfast at this Greek diner in my neigh-borhood.

"You sure you're up to it?" I asked.

"Absolutely," Keith said. "I'll need it tomorrow more than ever."

"All right," I said. "Tomorrow, then."

Without another word, Keith nodded at Josie and turned to his parents. A second later, Josie and I were on our way out, making our way past the Trinity fans for a final time.

"Wow," Josie said.

"What?"

"I don't know . . ." She flashed me this really affectionate smile. "You were so sweet to him back there."

"Oh?"

"I like a guy who's good to his friends."

Good to his friends? Yeah, that was me—in spades. Suddenly, I needed some air—big-time.

"These Trinity dweebs are beginning to bug me," I said. "Let's get out of here."

Eleven

The walk to Josie's—just ten blocks down Third Avenue to 65th Street—made me feel even worse. You see, it seemed that she wasn't simply impressed by how nice I had been to Keith—she was *really* impressed. I mean, she wouldn't shut up about it. To her I was this caring, mature person. Yeah, that was me all right. As mature as your average infant. The way I saw it, I had spent the past year reliving my terrible twos. Sure, I had felt momentarily happy for Keith after his show. And boy, had I ever felt bad for him when he blew those foul shots. But the bottom line was this: I was still an envious little sucker with the highest J.Q. in town.

And as Josie and I strolled down Third Avenue, I got to thinking about it some more:

Was it really possible that Keith screwed up because I'd wished it? Or that Wendie dumped him for a girl because of me? With those thoughts knocking around the old cranium what I really wanted to do was to just go home and worry in the privacy of my own room.

The trouble was that by the time Josie and I reached her apartment, I had to pee like you wouldn't believe. Like one of those horses in Central Park who just lets loose and seems to go forever. That was me. It was either go up to Josie's apartment or find a fire hydrant.

"Uh, hey . . ." I began.

(This was at her front door.)

"Yeah?" Josie said shyly.

Looking back, I think she probably thought I was about to ask for another date. Or maybe even go for a kiss. Boy, did she look surprised—and I think a little disappointed—when I asked if I could check out her facilities.

She said yes, of course. I mean, what else was she going to say? Still, I felt sort of funny on the elevator. See, I was worried that she might think I was just *saying* I needed to pee as an excuse to get inside her door. Like some real smooth operator. Which, as I'm sure you know by now, I'm not. Neither smooth nor highly operational. But

Josie didn't know that, right? And the trouble was, once I was upstairs, how could I prove that I really had needed to go? Leave a urine sample in one of her mom's wineglasses? Don't think so.

Josie's apartment was a nice place, actually, fairly spacious for New York. At first I could've sworn we were alone. But after using the bathroom, I followed Josie's voice down the hall. She was talking to a woman I assumed was her mom, though she looked awfully young.

"Hi, Matt," she said. "I'm Mrs. Hyde."

As we shook hands I noticed that, up close, she looked a bit older. Late thirties, maybe. Anyway, Mrs. Hyde's age isn't important. What is important is that for five minutes we successfully executed some polite Mom-friend chitchat and then, like all good mothers, she made some excuse (book to read) and beat a hasty retreat. Which left Josie and me alone.

Was I excited? Sure, I was.

Was I terrified? Sure, I was.

I mean, we were *alone*. In the living room. Since my bladder problem had been taken care of and since that was, after all, the reason I had come up to the apartment, I thought the tactful thing to do would be to leave. But Josie had other ideas.

"Wanna watch some TV?"

"Uh, sure," I said.

Hey, why not? I like TV.

"I think we have some brownies and soda in the kitchen. Want some?"

"Sure," I said.

Hey, I like them too.

"Wanna hump like a couple of rabid mountain goats?"

"Love to."

Okay, okay—questions one and two were real. Number three . . . well, that was just a thought that galloped across my brain while Josie flicked on the TV and went to the kitchen for the goodies. To tell the truth, I don't know where I got it from. Humping like rabid mountain goats seemed a little out of my league. Not to mention maybe even painful. I mean, they do it outside, on jagged rocks and at high altitude. No, I didn't want to hump like a rabid goat. Just kiss like a rabid teenager. Was that too much to ask?

Anyway, when Josie left the room I tried to clear my mind of goats and kissing by browsing the bookshelves. But there wasn't much interesting. Besides, I was too jittery to read—even a book called *Loving the Female You* I saw on an upper shelf. So that's when I decided to focus on something I could handle—

something to get my mind off the fact of my terrifying yet exciting aloneness with Josie: the TV.

Yes! The solution!

Uh, guess again. Directly in front of the set was a love seat. A sofa built for two. A make-out couch. And boy, as I looked that thing up and down, I nearly lost it. I'll tell you, it was definitely the first time in my life I felt intimidated by a piece of furniture. The way I was thinking, if I sat in it, I had to make out whether I wanted to or not. Don't get me wrong: I wanted to. But now that I was faced with the opportunity to do some serious kissing I felt scared of it—so scared that I thought it might be best to avoid the whole thing by plopping my butt down in the armchair next to the love seat. That way, unless Josie decided to crawl into my lap, I'd be safe. And then I wouldn't have to worry about the things a guy like me can worry about. Like being rejected. Or being a bad kisser. Or suddenly getting hard. I mean, I know that having sex is the ultimate goal of kissing but I'm not embarrassed to admit that I didn't think I was ready for it. The more I got to thinking about everything that could go wrong, the better the armchair looked. I probably would've wimped out completely and sat in the thing if I hadn't suddenly thought of what Keith would say if I did.

Something like: "Dude!!!! No way!!!!"

And he would've been dead-on right. No two ways about it. I had to be a man! I mean, just because I sat in the love seat didn't mean anything *had* to happen. Last I heard, a piece of furniture couldn't be electrically wired to force two people to make out, right?

Just sit! I told myself. *Sit!*

So I sat.

But two seconds later I was back on my feet. That's because Josie called, "Hey, Matt," from the kitchen and I jumped up like someone had stuck a cattle prod in my ear.

"Yeah?" I squeaked.

"Coke or root beer?"

"Root beer," I called, which is funny because I like Coke better. I tell you, I really wasn't thinking straight. "You need help?"

"Nah," Josie said. "I'll just be a second. Have a seat and relax."

Have a seat and relax? Oh, sure. To kill time, I paced the room about a million times. I considered climbing the bookshelves to grab *Loving the Female You* after all. But in the end I got so fed up with being a wreck that I just sat down—in the damned love seat, too. To kill time I tried watching the tube. But wouldn't you know it? The volume was down low and I couldn't find the remote! After I took what seemed like about ten minutes deciding whether to look for it or not, Josie reappeared and set a tray of brownies and the two sodas on the coffee table. Then she plopped herself down next to me like she had had years of love-seat experience. I mean, she didn't seem nervous at all. She handed me the root beer and took a Coke for herself.

"Cheers," she said and clinked her can to mine.

"Cheers," I replied.

I took a sip. Definitely should've gone for that Coke.

"Hey," Josie said, glancing toward the TV. "Why's the volume so low?"

Luckily, she spared me having to blurt out some idiotic answer. That's because on screen was a picture of an overturned sports car by the side of a road.

"Wait," Josie said. "Looks like someone famous got in an accident."

Turned out she was right. Josie found the remote in about two seconds and pumped up the volume. And the announcer was saying:

"We are now confirming reports that Sandra Millicent, recently voted *People* magazine's most beautiful woman of the year, lost control of her Porsche this afternoon on a Los Angeles freeway heading for the set of her latest film project. We now take you live to the hospital."

What?!?!?!?!?!

I felt my heart drop all the way down to my toes. I mean, this was *Sandra Millicent,* star of Keith's father's movie!!

"Oh, my God!" I gasped.

"Are you a big fan of hers?" Josie asked.

I was too stunned to attempt an answer. Back on the TV, the picture changed to the facade of an L.A. hospital. A newscaster, some young woman, was reporting from the scene.

"According to doctors at Los Angeles County Hospital, Sandra Millicent is one very lucky lady. Although there is no life-threatening injury, she has suffered facial lacerations and will have to undergo plastic surgery. It is unclear at this time how her legendary looks will be affected and whether she . . ."

I stopped listening. I tell you, I was close to nonfunctional. First, Wendie kisses a girl. Then, Keith muffs two easy free throws. And now this? Sandra Millicent! Needs plastic surgery? What had I said that night after the cast party? That I wished she'd turn into a horse? Or look like a horse? Something like that.

"Hey," Josie said. "You okay?"

Far from it. I felt totally creeped. Like the entire world was suddenly out of whack. But could I tell Josie what was going on? Of course I couldn't.

"Nothing," I managed. "I'm fine."

"Sandra'll be okay," Josie said sympathetically. "It's only a little plastic surgery."

I'm mortified to tell you what happened next. But I have to. You've got to remember how scared I was all of a sudden. How freaked out. I know it's okay for a thirteen-year-old boy to cry. But, still, it's not something you want to go out of your way to do, especially when you're with a girl you like, alone in her apartment on a love seat. Whatever. I just couldn't help it. Not that I was blubbering or anything. Just a few tears, rolling down my cheeks. But put yourself in my shoes! Suddenly, the whole wish thing was making terrible sense! Not only had I screwed up things for Keith—I had put a famous movie star in intensive care!

"Don't worry," Josie said. "She's going to be all right."

"I know," I sighed. "But . . ."

"But what?"

I looked her in the eye. Her face was about two inches from mine. Maybe closer.

"But Sandra Millicent was going to star in Keith's dad's movie," I cracked.

With that, I sort of hung my head low.

Which is when I heard Josie say, "My God, Matt. You are *so* sensitive."

She took my hand. Then I felt her other hand on the back of my head, rubbing my hair.

"I love how much you care for people. It's sweet."

Oh, no! She thought I was crying because I was upset for Keith! Of course, if I had been anything resembling human I would've spilled the beans right there. But I was too confused. And before I could collect my thoughts, I felt Josie gently lift up my face. When our eyes met we were about an inch apart. And just like that she leaned forward and kissed me really slow and gentle on the lips. I was too stunned to respond. I mean, I'd been kissed before—but not like that, so sweet and slow. And then she did it again. And then . . . well, then I started to kiss back.

Next thing I knew it was official. I was making out! And no kissing game, either. Josie was there of her own free will, cuddled up in my arms. Though Keith, Wendie, and Sandra Millicent were on my mind for the first minute or two, it didn't take long before I forgot all about them.

"You know," Josie told me, after fifteen minutes or so of Class A lip-o-suction, "you're the first guy I've ever really made out with. I mean, except for in kissing games."

"Wow," I said. "Me, too—exactly."

That news seemed to make her happy.

"You're a great guy," she said. "I like you."

"I like you, too," I said.

So it wasn't the suavest response. But it sure seemed all right with Josie. Because she said, "Come here," and pulled me toward her for another round. Which is when I realized something: Choosing that love seat was the best decision I had made in my entire life.

What in the world had made me so scared of it in the first place?

Twelve

Most mornings when I finally decide I'm awake enough to motivate, I'm up and out of the sack pretty fast. But the next morning was different. Because when a guy like me has a girl like Josie on his mind he gets to feeling so good that he's got to just lie there and think. Not to be overly mathematical about something so romantic or anything but, hey, Josie and I had made out for forty-six minutes!!!! (I know because I glanced at a clock on her mantel.) Not to mention the five more (untimed— no visible clock) at her front door before I left. Now, fifty-one minutes of kissing may not seem like a lot to someone with previous make-out experience. But in I'm-a-short-thirteen-year-old-loser years it was practically forever. I mean, FIFTY-ONE LIP-SMACKING

MINUTES!!! In light of that, who gave an otter's butt about anything else? Don't get me wrong—I still felt guilty about my wishes and all the stuff that had happened to Keith. I just sort of gave myself permission to put it on the back burner for a while.

But it wasn't long before I remembered my date with Keith at Nick's diner. Which made me realize something: After a full year of having heard about Jane and Allison and Barbara and Lynn and every other girl in the universe, it was finally *my* turn to be the guy with news! Yeah, I hadn't gotten to third base. Not even second. But that didn't mean I couldn't spread the word, right? I mean, what was the good of making out if you couldn't tell someone?

Anyway, I was pumped. So pumped that I jumped out of bed, dunked my Nerf basketball, pulled on some clothes, and headed for the front door. Which is when Mom cut me off at the pass, wanting to know *everything* about my date. Like what Josie was wearing and what she had for dinner and then all about the game and whether Josie liked it and whether I walked her home. On and on and on. I mean, it was so bad I half expected her to ask if Josie had a cute butt. But that wasn't even the worst of it. See, as soon as Mom was through, Dad appeared. And that's when things got really ugly.

You see, the trouble with having open-minded parents is that once every couple of months they love having what my dad calls these "little talks" when they get off telling me the sort of stuff you don't want to be talking about with anyone over fifteen. And always in the hokiest ways. I mean, the last time they did it my dad took off his glasses, looked at me all seriously and said, "making love to a woman is the most beautiful thing in the world." Uh, barfbag, please! I mean, I grant him the point. But did he really think that I didn't know that already? What did he think I was? Hormone deficient? Besides, his terminology bugged me. "Making love" made it sound too gushy—like something people did in bad TV movies. I preferred "having sex" or "doing it." Then again, if Dad ever said something like "Naked chicks rock!" I might not have liked that, either. Anyway, this wasn't a subject a guy wants to spend a Saturday morning discussing with his parents.

And now . . . well, Dad had *that look* on his face. No doubt about it—I had to get out and fast. So just as he was gearing up, I glanced at his watch.

"Sorry," I said. "I'm late!"

"Hey," he said. "What's the rush?"

"Gotta meet Keith!"

With that, I was out the door in seconds flat.

Talk about a close call!

Once I hit the street I was so eager to tell Keith what I wouldn't tell my parents that I ran the whole three blocks up to 75th and Lexington. I mean, I don't think I'd been this pumped to tell him something since . . . well, maybe since that time I'd nailed this older guy with a dozen Kool-Aid balloons from my terrace. And that was in fifth grade! But this was much better than Kool-Aid balloons!

This was sex!!!!

I was Matt Greene . . .

The Make-Out Meister!!!

King of the Fifty-One Minutes!!!!!!!

THE LIP-SUCKING GOD!!!!!!!!!!!!!!!!!

YES!!!!!!!!!!!!!!!!!!!!!!!!!!!!!!

Through the window I saw Keith sitting in our usual corner booth. He was already ordering. So I tapped on the glass, waved, then made for the door. Seconds later, I was seated across from him.

"Two over easy with bacon and a glass of OJ," I told the waiter. Then to my buddy:

"Dude!"

"Dude!" he said.

Now, when you've known a guy as long as I've known Keith you can tell a lot about his mood in a word or two. To someone who didn't know him, Keith's "dude" may have sounded like the "dude" of a perfectly happy guy. But to a close friend, Keith's "dude" had a hollow ring.

"What's up?" I asked.

"Ah, still bumming about Wendie, I guess," Keith said.

When I heard the name "Wendie" I sucked in this big breath and sort of held it. Of all possible topics, this was the toughest. I still didn't know what Keith knew about her. Even worse, I hadn't decided what to tell him if the subject came up. I mean, I had thought about it on the walk from the Empire Szechuan to the basketball game. But thinking and deciding are two different things, right? As it was, the whole thing made me uneasy—especially since I still had this vague idea that my wishes had some-thing to do with it.

"She was supposed to meet me at the game."

"You never heard from her?"

Keith forced a smile. "Yeah—this morning."

"She called?"

Keith sighed. "Nah . . . It's more pathetic than that. I called her—at nine."

"Wow . . . that early?"

Keith slid the salt shaker from one hand to the other a couple of times.

"I think I woke up her whole family."

"What'd she say?" I asked.

"What'd she say?" Keith repeated. "Well, according to her, she was all psyched to meet me last night. In fact, she was on the way out to the game when her dad came home and said that she had to hang with this uncle of hers who was in from Seattle." He shook his head. "Can you believe it? Talk about lousy timing!"

I didn't know whether to laugh or to cry. Her *uncle from Seattle?* I mean, unless that was the new lesbian slang, it didn't look like Wendie had been all that forthcoming.

"Uncle from Seattle, huh?" I said.

I was off the hook—at least for another two seconds.

"That's what she told me, anyway," Keith said. "Why? Don't you think she was telling the truth?"

"Well, why shouldn't she?" I stammered. "I mean, people have uncles, right? I'm sure it's nothing."

Okay, so I was a coward. Besides, Keith didn't seem like he wanted to know, anyway. At least that's how I justified it to myself. Still, it didn't take more than a millisecond before I got to feeling bad. The fact was this: Just because Keith *didn't* want to know about Wendie didn't mean that he *shouldn't* know. I mean, sometimes a person has to hear something even if it's bad, right? And sometimes a person has to tell someone something bad even if he doesn't want to. Bottom line: If the situation were reversed, I'd sure want Keith to be the one to break the news—not some sneering jerk who had heard it through the grapevine.

The next thing I knew I said, "Uh, Keith?" and he said, "Yeah?" and there was no turning back. Still, I wasn't quite sure what to say next. I mean, how do you break the unbreakable? Somehow I didn't think that saying, "Hey! Wendie Culhane's gay!" was the right approach.

"Listen," I said. "I think you should know something. Something I saw last night."

Boy, was my heart pounding. That's because I knew Keith would be upset. But also because I was still worried that the whole thing might be my fault.

"Yeah?"

"About Wendie."

Now it was my turn to play with the salt shaker. Man, was I nervous!

"What about her?"

"I saw her."

Well, that got Keith's interest.

"You saw her?! Where?"

"At the Empire Szechuan."

"Wait," Keith said. "She was at Empire Szechuan . . . with her *uncle?*"

"Uh, not exactly," I stammered.

"Then with who?" Keith asked.

"A friend," I managed.

"A friend?" Keith said. Now he looked alarmed. I don't think it had occurred to him that Wendie might have lied. "Some guy?"

"Actually, no," I said. "A girl."

Boy, did Keith's eyes go wide.

"A girl?"

"Right," I said.

I hoped that would be enough info to get the point across. Turned out it wasn't. That's because Keith totally misunderstood what I was trying to say!

"Thank God," he said. He settled back in his seat. "For a minute I thought you were going to tell me that she was seeing someone else."

Would this never end?

"Keith," I said. "She *is* seeing someone else."

"She is?" he asked. "What're you trying to say? Like, Wendie and this girl were kissing or something?"

120

He was kidding, of course. But I guess the look on my face told him pretty fast that it was no joke. There was this horrible, drawn-out pause. Then Keith said, "No!"

I nodded.

"No," he said again.

I nodded again, then started from the beginning and told him exactly what I had seen. I mean, I had to do it. And boy, was Keith shocked. With each word he sank lower and lower in his seat. And then, when I was through, he said, "I can't believe it" about fifty times, plus a mad flurry of "no ways!" Over and over and over. It was hard to take. But what made it even *harder* was Keith suddenly saying, "Just what I need . . . on the same night Sandra Millicent goes and drives into a concrete wall!" Boy, did *that* get my attention! Because after a few questions I got it out of him that filming on *The Asparagus Itch* was going to be delayed for a while. I don't know why I was surprised. I mean, the news had said Sandra M. needed plastic surgery. They couldn't expect a movie star to show up to the set with her face wrapped in gauze, right?

"Sorry, Keith," I said, feeling weird. He was so low, I thought he was going to break in two. "The whole thing sucks out loud. But Sandra will be okay. And Wendie? Just forget her.

She's too old, anyway. And conceited, too. A real princess!"

I went on like that for a while. I mean—anything to make Keith feel better. And after a while it began to pay off a bit. By the time the food arrived, Keith was halfway human and we were able to concentrate on our breakfast. But there's no explaining timing. Right when I was down to my last scrap of bacon, Keith drained his OJ and suddenly asked me the exact question my parents had wanted to know so badly. The one I had been waiting to hear from the very second I'd entered the diner.

"So you never told me what happened with Josie."

But, boy! What a difference a half an hour can make! I mean, on the way over, there had been nothing I'd wanted more than to share the big news. But how could I do that now? Wasn't it in poor taste to gush about your own good fortune when the person you're gushing to is miserable?

"Come on," Keith said. "Out with it."

"Well . . . ," I stammered.

"Don't be shy, dude."

I couldn't help myself.

"Well, Josie invited me back to her place . . ."

"Yeah?"

I spilled it.

"And we made out for fifty-one minutes!"

Keith blinked.

"Really?" he said.

"Really!" I said.

All of a sudden, I was practically giddy. And Keith? Just like that his face lit up with this enormous smile.

"Whoa!" he said. "Great news! Come on. Rewind to the beginning and tell me everything!"

So I did. And in the course of telling him about my fifty-one minutes in paradise, I realized something significant. For the first time in years . . .

I was the one doing well!!!

Matt Greene!!!

Top dog!!!

Make-out MEISTER!!!!!

YESSSSSS!!!!!!!!!

Talk about a good feeling!

Now promise not to hate me but for a couple of seconds I took that good feeling a step further. I actually *enjoyed* the fact that I was on top and Keith wasn't, that Keith's life had become a walking disaster area. Horrible, huh? Maybe. But don't forget: I had spent a lifetime living in my pal's shadow. It felt good to step out into the sunshine and watch him suffer, you know?

But then I was blindsided by this mega guilt wave.

"Dude!" Keith said as we were divvying up our money to pay the check. "Fifty-one minutes! Awesome!"

He looked majorly happy for me. Which made me wonder how I could be glad—even for a couple of seconds—that my best friend was screwing up. Especially when it was probably my fault! I needed to sort out my feelings and fast. But with who? The guy I'd usually talk to was the one I wanted to talk about!

"Say," Keith said as we hit the street. "Wanna shoot some hoops? Help me work on my foul shots?"

I hesitated.

"Come on," he said. "Help me take my mind off Wendie."

Under normal circumstances the answer would've been yes. But see, I had made a decision.

"Love to," I said. "But uh . . . my mom needs me at home. Supposed to clean my room. Then more guitar practice."

"I'm onto you, Greene," Keith said. "You're going straight back to Josie's to work on minute number fifty-two."

Boy, was I embarrassed that I'd admitted keeping one eye on the clock.

"I wish," I said. "Anyway—hang in there. I'll catch you later, okay?"

"Yeah, later."

"Later."

I watched him disappear around the corner of 75th Street, then made for the nearest pay phone and dialed information. Hey, don't forget—Derrick and I had just begun to hang out. I didn't have his number memorized yet.

Thirteen

"Hey, Derrick!"

"Matt? Where are you?"

"The corner of 75th and Lex. Listen, I need to talk!"

"What's going on?"

I wish I could say that I took a deep breath and told Derrick everything in a cool sort of way. But that would be one of the bigger and fatter lies of my life. Once the guilt started to come it backed up on me really fast. I was so stressed out that it all poured out in this mad rush. And to top it all off, just that moment his mom or dad or somebody started vacuuming, which made it nearly impossible for him to really hear. I mean, it was sort of comic if you want to know the truth. I was borderline hysterical and he was borderline deaf.

"What's going on?" I cried. "I've been up to my ears in weirdness, that's what! I think these wishes might be coming true. I saw Wendie Culhane cheating on Keith—with a girl!"

"A who?"

"A girl!" I shouted. "And when I was at Josie's the news said that Sandra Millicent had been in a car wreck!"

"Josie's cheating on Wendie?"

"No!" I shouted. That stupid vacuum! "Listen! I think those wishes came true. Do you hear what I'm saying, Derrick?" I was screaming into the phone. "TRUE!!!"

I finally got through to him. There was this pause on the other end of the line. Then the vacuum finally stopped.

"True?" Derrick said. "You mean your wishes?"

"Yes!" I said, relieved.

"Sounds like a coincidence to me."

"Keith screwing up a foul shot is a coincidence! But all the other stuff . . . it's just too much at once! Listen—can I come over? I need a place to think."

"Sure, sure. But what happened with you and Josie?"

"First things first," I said. "What's your address?"

I had him repeat it three times to make sure I remembered. Luckily, he lived nearby at 72nd and Madison. I hung up the phone and took off.

As fast as I had run to Nick's earlier that day, I ran even faster now. Say the words "basket case" ten times without inhaling and you'll get a pretty good insight into my mental state. I suddenly felt so bad about Keith's screwups that I half expected radioactive waste to start squirting out of my ears. So bad that by the time I arrived at Derrick's house I was too jumpy to sit. And Derrick could tell I was in serious trouble. Yeah, he asked one question about what had happened with me and Josie but I shot him such an intense "not now" look that he got me a cold glass of water and led me straight to his room.

"Come into my office," he said, and pushed open a door off the front hallway.

Remember I heard he lived in a closet? Turned out I heard it right. Apparently, Derrick had taken this coatroom off the main hallway to avoid having to share a bedroom with his younger brother. It seemed pretty extreme but, then again, I had never met his brother. The coatroom was large as closets go but real small for a room. Still, I had to admire what Derrick had done with the limited space. The walls were covered with *Star Trek* posters. And by covered, I mean *covered*. There were Kirks, Spocks, Picards, Datas, Klingons, Romulans, and Ferengi everywhere you looked. But that wasn't all. See, Derrick had attached these glow-in-the-dark stars to his ceiling. I like sci-fi and all, but well, with the room so tiny and those stars on the ceiling, a guy could begin to feel like he was orbiting the third moon of Saturn or something. If there had been room to pace, I would've paced. As it was, I was so wound I immediately started to fidget with this Dr. McCoy doll on Derrick's dresser.

"Okay," Derrick said from his bed. "Now take a deep breath, relax, and tell me everything. And I mean everything. But this time—slowly."

I did my best, I swear I did. I mean, my descriptions were still what Mr. Freyer, my English teacher, would have called "melodramatic." But eventually I got all the important info across. When I was done, Derrick lay back and looked at the ceiling.

"It's a toughie," he said finally.

"What do you mean 'a toughie'?"

"Well," he said. "For starters we can't be sure whether your wishes are what caused all this stuff or not."

"I suppose."

"But if they are," Derrick went on, propped up on one elbow now, "there's only one thing I can think of to do."

"What? Tell me!"

"Easy! Find the homeless guy and ask him to reverse the spell."

"Find the homeless guy?" I said.

"Right!"

For a split second I got pretty caught up in the idea. Yeah, it was far out. But at least it was a plan, right? Derrick and I would find the guy, buy him a sandwich or something, ask him to undo my wishes, and then BAM!— order would be restored! Yes!!!!

"Sounds great," I said. "Let's get going."

But wait!

I mean, what was I thinking? New York has about ten thousand million people in it.

"Ah, forget it," I said. "Our guy could be anywhere. For all we know, he got together some money and caught a bus to Peru."

With those words I sank onto Derrick's bed and began to wallow in this sort of sick self-pity. I felt suddenly as though I'd been possessed by some weird aliens using me as a vessel to destroy my best friend. Don't ask me why these aliens wanted him destroyed—I didn't get that far. The point is that for about five seconds I was absolutely convinced of it.

And lemme tell you, when you're thinking something that freaky, five seconds can seem like forever. Luckily, I was saved by a voice back on planet Earth: a mom.

"Derrick!" she called. "Derrick!"

Next thing I knew she was rapping on the door.

"Yeah?" Derrick said.

"Sorry to interrupt. But isn't it your turn to take out the trash?"

Derrick rolled his eyes. "Can't it wait?"

"Please, honey! It's stinking up the kitchen."

We heard her footsteps walking away. Derrick sighed, then in one motion rose to his feet and kicked open his door, flooding the room with light. His mom was in the living room, straightening magazines on the coffee table.

"I tied it up for you."

"Come on," Derrick said to me. "We'll continue this conversation in the park."

Ten minutes later, he and I sat on a bench by this man-made lake at 72nd Street. It's not a big lake or anything—more like a basketball court across and a football field long. To be honest I began to feel pretty humiliated during the walk over there. I mean, I was a kid who normally had his head screwed on straight. I had outgrown magic wishes back in first grade and stopped believing in Santa in second. Had I really almost agreed to hunt down a magical street person? I mean, talk about *whacked!* In fact, I was feeling too whacked to talk at all. Instead, I watched a kid get on his knees and put a toy boat in the water. Suddenly I wished I was him. Or his boat, even. Or a mouse on the stupid boat—like that scene in the book *Stuart Little.* See, that's how bad off I felt. Willing to trade my life for a rodent's.

"I've been doing some thinking," Derrick said finally.

I guess he realized that if he waited for me to talk he'd be looking at a couple of millenniums down the road.

"Oh?" I said.

"Yeah . . . the way I figure it you've got two options."

"I do?"

"One, we go for it and look for the street guy."

I sighed. "Like I said, we'll never find him."

"True."

"So what's number two?"

Derrick shrugged. "Easy. Just forget the whole thing."

"Forget the whole thing?" I said.

He stood up and tossed a tiny stick into the water.

"You heard me. Sure, Keith gets so many babes it's disgusting. Enough to make a guy sick. And he has been a little full of himself lately." Derrick turned to face me. "Hey, if he were *my* best friend I'd get a little jealous of him now and then too. Still, there's no way on this planet—and remember this is from a guy who lives for science fiction—that your wishes are what's making Keith screw up. Matt, you're obsessing."

"You think?" I said.

"Yeah," Derrick said. "Keith's just going through a rough patch. Happens to everybody. In another week he'll be back on top of the world."

He picked up a stone and skipped it across the lake. I watched it bounce three times, then ripple into the water.

"Yeah," I said. "Maybe you're right."

"Whatever," he said, sitting back next to me. "But enough of this Keith garbage. We have more pressing things to discuss."

"We do?" I said. "What?"

Derrick smiled.

"Commander Spock from planet Vulcan bids you speak! What happened with Josie?"

"God," I said. "If I didn't know better I'd say you had a crush on her."

Derrick's eyes went wide. "Me? On Josie? Nah!"

I'd been joking, of course. But his "nah" wasn't all that convincing. Hey, he and Josie were good friends, right? Suddenly, the whole crush idea didn't seem so far out.

"Well, do you?" I asked.

Derrick kicked another stone into the lake and sighed.

"The truth?"

I nodded.

"At the beginning of the year, yeah," he said. "But now it's just friends."

"Really?"

"Really."

Then he looked embarrassed.

"What?" I said.

"To be honest, I sort of think Sheila's cute."

Whoa! This was news!

"DeCappio?"

He nodded. "That's the one."

Sheila DeCappio was that girl standing with Josie at the cast party. The one with the blond streaks I had written the African mammal paper with back in fourth grade. I didn't know her all that well but she and Derrick seemed like a good fit. They both had weird hair, anyway.

"I had no idea," I said. "Why don't you ask her out?"

Derrick shrugged. "Aw, I don't know."

"Come on," I said. "Why not?"

He paused. "Well . . . I mean, look at me, Matt. She probably doesn't know I'm alive—I mean, in a boyfriend sort of way."

Life is so funny. Suddenly I was like Keith, the guy with experience.

"Come on," I said. "She'll like you. Hey, you're a cool guy."

He shrugged again. "Yeah," he said. "Whatever."

"Tell you what," I said as the idea came to me. "If I tell you about what happened with Josie, you have to promise to go back home and call Sheila."

"Call Sheila?" Derrick said. "Now? No way."

"Yes way! Ask her out!"

You should've seen it. Derrick suddenly looked like a cornered dog.

"Ah, I don't know . . ."

"You'll never know if you don't try, right?" I stuck out my hand. "Come on. Shake on it."

To tell the truth, I put the odds of his accepting my proposition at about twenty jillion light-years to one. But I suppose life can be weirder than science fiction sometimes. Because before I knew it, my new pal had clasped my hand.

"All right," he said. "It's a deal."

"Hey! That's great. Now remember, right after I tell you about—"

"Yeah, yeah," Derrick said, waving me off. "I go home and call Sheila. But your story better be worth it. Now, let's start from the beginning. . . . So the basketball game is over. How'd you manage to get up to her apartment afterward?"

I grinned, remembering.

"Derrick," I said, stretching back on the bench. "I couldn't have found a better way upstairs if I'd tried!"

Fourteen

Stop obsessing, huh?

That's what Derrick had said, right?

Well, easier said than done. I mean, have you ever heard of a botched nose job? It's supposed to be a basic operation, isn't it? Not easily screwed up. Especially when the nose in question belongs to a movie star!

Hold on a minute and you'll see what I mean. See, after I walked Derrick home from the park (he promised he was going to keep up his side of the bargain and call Sheila ASAP), I passed this newsstand on the corner of 74th and Lexington. And that's where the botched nose job comes in. Because there she was— Sandra Millicent—smack on the cover of the *Post!*

And guess what?

THE WOMAN LOOKED LIKE A HORSE!

Don't believe me? Well, check out the head-
line:

SANDRA SEZ: NEIGH! NEIGH!

And one rack over was the *Daily News!*

SANDRA'S NOSE:
NO WIN, PLACE, OR SHOW!

I wish I could say I took it in stride. But I
was so bowled over I had to lean against a car
to keep my balance. I was weak at the knees.
Don't forget: "Looks like a horse" was one of
my wishes!

No more obsessing?

Yeah, *right!*

Suddenly my obsessions had obsessions!
Seriously. Those papers put me back in "I-
screwed-over-my-best-buddy" guilt mode faster
than you could shout "Sandra Secretariat!"

And when I finally collected myself enough
to stumble toward home, it was like I had no
mental control. I tortured myself half to death
with this horrible stream of Keith-related fan-
tasies. Crazy things like my best bud getting
tossed out of school for cheating. Or breaking
his legs in a freak boating accident. I even

imagined him contracting a severe case of elephantiasis and having to live out the rest of his life on a diet of baked peanuts in a commune in Bolivia. Even worse, I could see the headlines:

TEENAGE DWARF HEXES BEAUTIFUL
BEST BUD NOW TURNED ELEPHANT!

By the time I got back to the apartment I was so upset I wouldn't have minded if Dad had wrapped me in a straitjacket and fed me some rhino tranquilizers. But there was no help on the home front.

"Hi, honey!" Mom said when I slumped through the door. "Guess what?"

"What?" I managed.

I was nervous. By that point I thought she was going to tell me Keith had contracted rabies from an infected pigeon or something.

"Miss Antonucci called," my dad said, joining us in the foyer.

"Oh?" I said.

Was I about to be accused of stealing a drawerful of her orange socks? Apparently not. Just then, Mom and Dad exchanged this "Gosh, we're proud" glance.

"You made the first cut for the Paris summer scholarship!" Mom said. "They want you to send a tape of two more pieces—one classical, one modern."

Now, under normal circumstances that would've been great news. I mean, after being deep-sixed by Aspen, I was still alive in France! But in my semi-deranged state that afternoon, my personal success only made me feel guiltier about Keith's disasters.

"Wow," I stammered.

"What's wrong?" Dad said. "You don't seem very excited."

That's the trouble with having a dad who's a shrink. You can't get away with feeling anything.

"Oh, I am," I said, covering for myself. "Really psyched. In fact, I think I'm going to my room to practice this very minute."

By the time I closed my door I had made a decision. No more feeling happy about my best bud's screwups. Especially when those screwups were likely my fault! No, it was time to do what was right. To do whatever it took to restore Keith to his former glory. You know, get him back where he belonged: with a babe on one arm, a sport's trophy in the other, and his face on a bus!

That was my plan, anyway. And I have to admit that I thought it was a pretty good one—for the next three seconds. That's because the more I thought about it the more

I saw that there was nothing—and I mean *nothing*—I could do to change the facts.

1. Foul Shots. Sorry. But Keith's air ball was history. Hannaford had lost the seventh-and-eighth-grade basketball championship fair and square. And, anyway, how could I possibly help Keith improve his free throw shooting? Like I said before, he was already hitting eighty percent—better than most pros.

2. Wendie Culhane. It'd never work. Here's me on the phone to her:

"Hello, Wendie? Matt Greene, Keith's friend. Now I hope you know that I fully support your desire to experiment with your sexuality—hey, my dad says that being a teenager is about breaking boundaries. But now that you've had your fun with your girlfriend, how about getting back into the heterosexual business?"

Can you imagine? She would've hung up the minute I said my name.

3. Sandra Millicent. I considered running an Internet search for a nose specialist. But I mean, who was I fooling? Sandra Millicent is a movie star. The best doctors in the world were probably lining up to fix her face—not to mention throw in a tummy tuck and an eye job to boot.

See? Three problems—three strikeouts.

Which really stunk. What I needed was to go back to square one and . . .

But then it hit me:

I had to find the street person and get him to reverse the wishes!

Okay, so it was crazy. Make that *really* crazy—an idea I had dismissed no more than an hour before with Derrick. And believe me, I still knew the odds. The guy could've been anywhere from Hoboken to living in a hut in Western Australia doing research on genetically engineered kangaroos. Not to mention the fact that I knew perfectly well that random street people don't have magical powers. For that matter, that *no one* has magical powers outside of a Harry Potter book.

Still, I had to try it. I mean, with my wishes weighing on my mind so hard I just had to know for sure. And by that point I was willing to try anything to help get my buddy's life back on track. It was time to act!

"Hey," I told my parents as I headed for the door. "I have to go out for a while."

"Wait a second," Dad called from the living room. "What about your practicing?"

"And don't you have a science test coming up?" Mom asked.

Arggghhhhh!

How could I think about Bach inventions or the periodic table when my friend's life was on the line?

I promised to be home by four.

Fifteen

But plans change, right?

See, the minute I ran out of my building, I caught a glimpse of something out of the corner of my eye—a bright red glint about three blocks down Second Avenue. When I raised my hand to block the sun, I saw that the red glint was a bike. And then I did this massive double take. That's because the rider was . . . Josie! And boy was she moving! Before I knew it, she hopped the curb and screeched to a halt by my side.

"Hi," I said. "You practicing for the Tour de France or something?"

Okay, so it wasn't the greatest joke. Not a joke at all really. Still, Josie smiled.

"Actually, I used to bike race in L.A."

"You did?"

She shrugged. "Yeah."

No doubt about it—I liked this girl. First, it was that backward Dodgers cap. Then it was her poem about old Cyrus Henry Merkle. Then the love seat. And now? Turned out she was a closet speedster!

"I was doing a loop of the park and thought I'd drop by." She leaned her bike against my building. Then she sort of wrinkled her brow. "I hope that's all right?"

"All right?" I said. "It's great!"

I mean, I couldn't remember the last time a friend had just "dropped by" without calling—and that included Keith. Maybe it was an L.A. thing. Maybe spending your whole life tan in a bathing suit makes you more casual about stuff like that? Whatever. The point is that Josie had come by to say hello. Which, like I said, was fantastic. But it also had this strange effect on us. Suddenly neither of us had a thing to say. It was weird. We had made out—a pretty intimate thing to do, right? But somehow Josie's "thought I'd drop by" seemed even *more* intimate, like we had crossed some sort of unwritten affection boundary.

"Hey," she said. "I heard from Sheila before I left. Turns out that Derrick called her."

"Oh, really?"

I know he'd said he was going to. But I guess I'd figured he wouldn't work up the guts.

"Apparently they really hit it off."

"Cool," I said. "What did they talk about?"

"Everything, I guess," Josie said. "I think it got pretty personal. You know, they really opened up to each other."

"Hey," I said. "That's great!"

Was I ever lying. Call me paranoid but just like that my heart was pounding like it was going to catapult right out of my chest and bunny-hop down the street. I knew full well what sorts of things Derrick might "open up" about. Things like a friend's wishes! Like I said, *paranoid*. But I was suddenly dead certain that the eighth-grade grapevine had kicked in full throttle. Which meant that Derrick had blabbed to Sheila! And Sheila had blabbed straight to Josie!

All of which could only mean one thing.

The reason Josie had dropped by wasn't to say hello. It was to dump my sorry butt! I mean, how could she go out with a guy who had wished his best friend would crash and burn? Sure, she was acting nice and all. But the ax was going to fall. I was sure of it.

"They make a cute couple," Josie said.

I felt weak at the knees. To tell the truth, I felt weak pretty much everywhere.

"They're going to see this band downtown," she went on. "But if they get carded, they'll catch a movie."

"Oh, really?" I choked out. "Sounds like fun . . ."

"So," she asked. "What're you doing tonight, anyway?"

Talk about a strange way to give someone the ax!

"Tonight? . . ." I said.

"Yeah," she said.

"I don't know," I said. "Studying and practicing, I guess."

"Studying and practicing?" Josie said. "Not on a Saturday night."

"No?"

Josie shook her head.

"Hey," I said. "What's wrong?"

"What's wrong?" she asked. Then she smiled, hands on her hips. "I guess I was hoping that we could do something."

I'm embarrassed to admit it but it was a good five seconds before I finally realized I wasn't getting dumped. And then . . . well, then I suddenly felt like the biggest moron this side of the third moon of Jupiter. I mean, talk about misreading a situation!

"I'm sorry," I said. "I had a great time last night. I should've asked."

147

"Oh, whatever!" Josie said. She suddenly looked super embarrassed. "I shouldn't have brought it up."

"No," I said. "It's my fault! Really!"

Then I got this idea. Something sort of cheesy but also sort of charming, maybe. If I could pull it off, that is.

"Listen," I said. "Tell you what . . . why don't we pretend that you never said a word about tonight, okay?"

Josie looked confused. "Never said a word? . . ."

"Yeah," I said. "Get back on your bike and ride up just like you were first arriving."

"Like I was just . . . ?"

"Yeah . . . could you?" I took her hand. "Please?"

Man, was Josie a good sport! I mean, once she bought into it, it was sort of amazing how fast she got into my little act. So it wasn't long before Josie was on her bike again, circling back down the block. Which gave me time to pick this yellow flower that was growing in a little plot by our front door. New Yorkers like to plant flowers. I knew they weren't for picking. But I figured this was for a good cause. I mean, what are flowers for, anyway, if not for love? Anyway, it wasn't long before Josie skidded to a halt by my side. And this time I was ready. When I held up that flower, she gasped—sort of like I had just pulled off this incredible magic trick or something. Yep, she was pretty charmed, I could tell. This elderly couple walked by and gave us a weird look like I was proposing or something. But I wasn't thinking about marriage. No, I wanted something much more modest.

"Josie?" I asked. "Would you like to do something tonight?"

She took the flower. Man, did she look happy. Girls are sort of like moms sometimes. They can be easy to please if you know what you're doing.

"I'd love to," she said.

"Great," I said.

Then I did something pretty suave. I kissed her hand. She giggled. I know for a certified fact that I was blushing, so I moved the conversation forward as fast as I could.

"How about calling Derrick and Sheila?" I asked.

"That'd be fun," Josie said. "But tonight's their first date, after all. We should leave them alone."

"Yeah," I agreed. "Then why don't we . . . I don't know . . ." I suddenly couldn't think of a single thing to suggest out of the million ideas spinning through my head.

"See a movie?" Josie said.

I smiled. "Sounds great."

And just like that—totally out of nowhere—Josie gave me this kiss on my lips. I glanced toward the lobby. Thank God the doorman was looking the other way and the parentals were upstairs!

"You're such a nice guy," Josie said.

I swallowed hard.

"Yeah," I said. "I guess . . . you, too. I mean, you're a nice girl. More than nice. Much more."

So I wasn't too good at the sweet talk. But hey, I was on the spot and it was all I could think of.

Neither of us knew what to say for a minute. I mean, it was like I actually had proposed. But guess who broke the silence? Again, not yours truly.

"Well, see you tonight then," Josie said.

"You got it. I'll pick you up around seven."

Next thing I knew, she was pedaling away fast. As I watched her move up to 74th, I got to thinking about how lucky I was to have met her. And not just plain old lucky . . .

I mean, REALLY, REALLY lucky!!!

A funny girl. A cool girl. Okay, a slightly weird girl. But a girl who liked me. Who trusted me. And the more I stood there thinking about how great Josie was, the more I began to feel awful all over again that I had made those stupid wishes. For a second, I felt even more determined to find that street person and put an end to all the craziness. Then I felt like running after Josie and confessing the whole sad story. I almost did, too. But I realized something—probably the most important thing I had realized that whole miserable week. If I really wanted to be worthy of Josie— to be the nice guy she thought I was—I didn't need to search for any magical street person I knew I'd never find and who wasn't magic in the first place. No, if I wanted to be worthy of Josie I had to be a man. You know, step up to the plate and face the music. Not confess to her. No, I needed to confess to the guy who really mattered:

To Keith.

My best bud.

Because it suddenly seemed clear that if I came clean to him about my raging J.Q.—you know, just honestly told him how I'd been feeling over the past year or so, maybe even apologize—I'd finally be able to put the whole embarrassing mess behind me.

Then who knew what would happen?

Maybe things would even get back to normal.

Sixteen

It was weird. But the minute I made the decision the rest was easy. As easy as digging into my pocket for a quarter, walking to the nearest pay phone, and dialing. My pal answered on the first ring.

"Hello?"

"Hey!" I said. "What's up?"

"My agent called when I got back from the diner this morning," he said. "Just got back from an audition. Some shampoo ad."

Talk about typecasting. It was perfect.

"Where will your picture be this time . . . if you get it, I mean?"

Keith paused. "You'll never believe it."

"Try me."

"The back cover of *Teen Life!*"

"No!"

"Yeah!"

"You're kidding!"

"Don't get too excited. I probably won't get it."

Maybe not, but it was still perfect. Keith's mouth had been on a bus. Why not his face on a magazine? Of course, given how things had been going they'd probably accidentally draw a gigantic piece of snot dangling out of his nose or something.

"But," he went on. "I did get something else!"

The minute he said it, I knew. I could hear that old Keith Livingston, King-of-the-World tone in his voice.

"Oh, no!" I said. "You've met somebody!"

"I'm back in business," he said. "I lined up a date for next week!"

"You dog," I said. "Where'd you meet?"

"At the audition."

"So she's a blonde, I guess?"

"Down to her waist."

"Did you check close to make sure she isn't actually one of the Hanson brothers?" I asked. "You may have a date with a teenage boy."

"Don't worry. I checked."

I was about to ask for more details. But then I remembered the real reason for the call.

Besides, there was only so long you could talk on one quarter. I could get the rest in person.

"Listen," I said. "Can I drop by? There's something I'd like to talk about."

"What?"

"Uh . . . tell you in person?"

Keith laughed. "Sure. Come on over. I'll be practicing guitar. You can give me a lesson." He paused. "Maybe teach me a fifth chord."

I laughed. "Sure," I said. "Glad to."

"Later, dude."

"Later."

You know those statues of Buddha you see around sometimes? The ones where he's sitting sort of Indian style, arms folded across his chest, with this look of supreme peace on his face like he's just won the Lotto or something? Or better yet, like he *hasn't* won the Lotto and is stone broke but is *so* relaxed that he doesn't care because he knows that he's going to end up in Nirvana, anyway? Well, I'm not saying I was feeling *that* good. And I'm sure not saying that I had any ticket for Nirvana. But by the time I'd hit Central Park on the way to Keith's I felt about as Buddha-like as I had in weeks. Which was surprising. I mean, given what I was on my way to do—tell my best friend that I had wished that his life would fall apart—you would've thought that I'd be shaking straight out of my high-tops. But I guess I was feeling relieved that the whole horrible ordeal was finally going to be over. I mean, let's face it—ever since the night I'd made those miserable wishes, guilt had been my middle name. I was aching to bare my soul. Besides, the more I thought about it, it was hard to imagine that Keith would be angry. No, he'd probably say something like:

"You thought your wishes screwed me up? Dude, how old are you, anyway? Five?"

Or, "Yeah, I was upset by those pictures of Sandra, too. But then I got to thinking. They were taken just after surgery, right? Soon as she heals she's going to be fine. You'll see."

Then he'd laugh and forget about it. See, my buddy was born able to take practically anything in stride—something I was still struggling to do.

Anyway, I was so eager to get the ball rolling that halfway across the park I began to jog a little bit. Which is when this final weird thing happened.

By that I mean: I saw him.

No, not Keith.

The street person. At least I *think* I saw

him. It was really just a flash of a gray beard and a wrinkled face out of my peripheral vision. It could have been anyone around fifty with raggedy clothes. Even so, I almost took off after him—almost demanded that he set my wishes straight. But I never really broke stride. That's right—I kept my bearings on my destination: Keith's place. The truth was I was too psyched about my life to care. Okay, maybe no one was going to develop an elevated J.Q. on my account anytime soon. But things weren't going too badly, right? I mean, I had a couple of good buddies, a shot at a scholarship to Paris, and a girlfriend.

What else did a five-foot-one-and-a-half-inch, guitar-playing thirteen-year-old nerd really need?

Not much.